ESCAPE THROUGH THE ANDES

ESCAPE THROUGH THE ANDES

A NOVEL

Thomas M. Daniel

2017 · Fithian Press, McKinleyville, California

Cover photograph by the author. Mount Mururata from the road to Palca, Bolivia, 1970.

Published by Fithian Press
A division of Daniel and Daniel, Publishers, Inc.
Post Office Box 2790
McKinleyville, CA 95519
www.danielpublishing.com

Distributed by SCB Distributors (800) 729-6423

LIBRARY OF CONGRESS CATALOGING-IN-PUBLICATION DATA
Names: Daniel, Thomas M., (date) author.
Title: Escape through the Andes : a novel / by Thomas M. Daniel.
Description: McKinleyville, California : Fithian Press, 2017.
Identifiers: LCCN 2017034210 | ISBN 9781564746023 (softcover : acid-free paper)
Subjects: LCSH: Intelligence officers—Fiction. | GSAFD: Adventure fiction. | Suspense fiction. | Spy stories.
Classification: LCC PS3604.A5256 E75 2017 | DDC 813/.6—dc23
LC record available at https://lccn.loc.gov/2017034210

For Janet, Ginnie, Steve, Laura, and Bruce,
who lived with me in Bolivia.

CONTENTS

ESCAPE THROUGH THE ANDES

PROLOGUE

FEET POUNDING ON COBBLES, breathing hard—panting and gasping—we rounded the corner and ducked into an alley. Our pursuers raced on past the alley. We had lost them. Escaped—for the moment.

"Whew!" Leaning forward with hands on my knees, I caught my breath. "That was close."

"Yeah!"

"But we've lost them, I think."

"*Esta vez*, but they'll keep after us."

"And we'll keep running!"

PART I

LA PAZ, BOLIVIA, 2007

1

I FOUND A CORNER TABLE in the bar at the Hotel Europa in La Paz. There were not many people in the bar. A middle-aged couple at a table across the room from me. A few well-dressed men at the bar, and one table with five similar men crowded around it. Businessmen, I judged. Well, I thought, that's what I am supposed to be—a businessman. I was wearing the dark blue suit in which I had traveled, minus the necktie. One of the young waitresses, suitably attired in a short dark skirt and white blouse and wearing spike-heeled shoes, approached me. Rosa Maria, by her name tag. *"¿A tomar?"* she asked.

"Sí. Un pisco sour." I replied, ordering the drink I was supposed to be drinking when my contact person appeared.

"Claro. Prontito. Of course. Right away." She went to the bar to get my drink for me.

I sipped my pisco sour, hoping to drag it out until my contact arrived. He should be along any minute, I thought. My watch said the 6:30 *rendez-vous* hour would soon be passed.

"¿Cacahuates?" asked Rosa Maria, as she put a small bowl of peanuts on my table. I took the peanuts, tossed a couple into my mouth, and squirmed in my seat. I wondered when and whether my contact, whoever he might be, would show up. And what would I do if he did not?

Rosa Maria returned with my check. *"Su cuenta, Señor. Firmamela, por favor."* As requested, I signed the check. *"El numero de su habitación,"* she said, pointing to a space on the bottom of the check. Room 414, I entered. Then, leaning close to my ear, she said softly in unaccented English, "I am your CIA contact person. I will come to your room just after seven-thirty, when my shift here ends." She took the signed check to the cashier and turned to assist another customer.

Well, I thought, that was slick. I ate a few more peanuts, finished my pisco sour, and headed up to my room.

PART II

CLEVELAND, OHIO, 2007

2

"PAUL? PAUL MORGAN?"

I turned in my chair. "Dave! For heaven's sake! What brings you here? What a surprise!" I rose to my feet and stuck out my hand to shake his. "Great to see you. But how come? I mean, welcome here."

"Am I intruding? Just busting in like this?"

"No, no. Of course not. Well, I have this grant proposal to finish up, but.... Anyway, the deadline is not until next week. Come in. Sit down." I pointed to the one side chair in my small office.

My office was indeed small, and there was only a single visitor chair—a scoop-shaped, black, plastic one. I am a professor of medicine at Case Western Reserve University (CWRU), based in the Department of Medicine at University Hospitals of Cleveland. I have a research program and a laboratory in the Wearn Research Building, a wing added onto the hospital. My office was intended to be a small instrument room for the laboratory. Since no other space was offered to me, I moved in a desk and established myself there. Mostly, however, I piled papers and unread journals on the desk and worked at what should have been an instrument counter along the back wall, which is why I hadn't seen Dave Swenson enter.

There were bookshelves above my desk-counter. There were no books on the bottom-most one of them—only piles of papers waiting for my attention. Taped to the walls were data tables and hand-drawn graphs and charts. Important stuff. Important to the grant renewal proposal upon which I was working when Dave arrived. Successful grant applications require not only good ideas but solid preliminary data. Solid, yes, but also sufficiently "cutting

19

edge" to excite a peer review panel of experts in one's field. Solid and cutting edge and hopefully exciting data from my laboratory were manifest in the tables and charts on my office walls. I was finding ways to include them in my proposal.

I study immune responses to the germ that causes tuberculosis (TB). How I became interested in this disease, a disease that is rapidly disappearing in the United States, is another story. I blame an army assignment taking care of soldiers with TB. That studies of this disease have taken me to parts of the world still plagued with the "Captain of Death" is yet another story. Having once set my sights on the disease that causes the most infectious disease deaths in the world, I found my innate wanderlust ready to take me to the parts of the world where TB lurks. My studies of tuberculosis have been and are tales of adventures told in stories of my research life, stories revealed in papers published in biomedical scientific journals. And stories recounted in proposals for grants in support of my work.

The human body has two sets of immune mechanisms for dealing with such unwanted invaders as disease-causing germs. Those mechanisms that are evoked by tubercle bacilli are prototypes for what immunologists call cellular responses. Cellular because they are mediated and effected by special cells as opposed to antibodies, which defend us against many other and more common infections. My laboratory-based studies of these cells and what they do when challenged in laboratory systems are complemented by studies in persons suffering from tuberculosis. And those latter, people-based studies have taken me to Bolivia. There is a lot of TB in Bolivia.

Dave Swenson had been my roommate at Yale. He had musical talent. He played the carillon in Harkness Tower. I trudged up the hill to the science buildings; I had no musical talent, although given enough beer, I enjoyed singing. While I followed graduation by going off to medical school at Harvard, Dave went to Georgetown for a graduate degree in International Affairs. He then took a job at the State Department, or so I understood. I was totally ignorant of what he did at the State Department.

I supposed he worked in Washington and maybe was assigned to other posts some of the time. Our Christmas card exchanges always went to his home in Virginia, however. Other than those Christmas cards, we had not kept in touch. Surprising, since we had been close college friends. But then life—at least my life—was busy, and so Christmas cards were all the contact I had maintained with most of my college classmates.

"What brings you to Cleveland? Hey, it's great to see you. Where are you staying? How long will you be in town?"

"Actually, I came to see you! I'm staying on your campus at the Glidden House. I go back to D.C. tomorrow."

"Well. I'd invite you to our house for dinner, but Susan is in Chicago for an art show—she has really made it in the art world—so there's just me at home at the moment. And I'm a terrible cook!"

"No problem. Let me take you out to dinner. Some place where we can talk."

"Fine by me. We'll go out, but it will be my treat."

"We can argue about that," Dave said. "But I have an expense account for this trip, so my bosses at the U.S. Gov. will treat us."

Jennifer, the senior one of the two technicians working my lab, came to the office doorway, paused for a moment, and said, "Sorry to interrupt. The gels are finished and in a tray to incubate overnight. Everyone else has left, and I'm headed out. Okay?"

"Yes. Sure. See you tomorrow."

"Good night. I will be a bit late tomorrow morning. My dog has developed a problem that is mysterious to me, and I need to take her to the vet."

"Okay. Have a good evening."

3

THE MAD GREEK is a Cleveland Heights landmark. It sits at the top of Cedar Hill, a short distance from University Hospitals and the CWRU campus. Susan and I live in Cleveland Heights, and we often patronize the Mad Greek. Serving both Greek and Indian food, it is a favorite restaurant of many of my fellow faculty members. Not crowded on most week nights, it is a place where one can eat leisurely and talk without too many intrusions by servers repeatedly asking if everything is satisfactory. The bar area can be noisy, but most of the restaurant area is not. We ordered, beginning with drinks. Scotch—Glenmorangie, no ice, water on the side, for Dave. A Tanqueray gin martini on the rocks with two olives for me.

"So, why... what... how come you are here?" I asked.

A waiter brought our drinks. We clicked glasses, and placed our dinner orders. Dave ordered dolmades. I chose a curry. And I ordered extra pita bread.

"Well," Dave began, "first of all, you have to know that I work for the CIA."

"Not the Culinary Institute of America," I interjected trying to leaven the conversation a bit.

"No, nowhere near Hyde Park. But, you know, I've been there. Had a great lunch there once. No, I work for the CIA that Baldacci, Child, Coulter, and their ilk write about. But it's not much like what they describe, you know. Mostly not very exciting. Anyway, I'm a spook. Not really, I do all my spy stuff at a desk, mostly with a computer. But at one time, I did do a little overseas stuff. Even that was mostly pretty mundane. Boring, really. But, you know, the CIA is important. We do a lot to protect this country.

"Next," Dave continued, "you have to understand that I know a lot about you. And then, you need to know that we have some problems in Bolivia that only you can help us with."

"Bolivia?"

"Yes, Bolivia. You spent a sabbatical year there back in 1981."

"Yeah, '81–'82. A long time ago."

"You've been back since, haven't you?"

"Well yes, several times," I replied. "If you are going to study TB, which is what I do, you can't do much of it in Cleveland—at least not any part of it that involves studying people. There just is not enough of it here. Well, of course, more tuberculosis would not be welcome, but if I want to study that disease, or any disease, I need to go to places where it occurs. In fact, I've been all over the world chasing TB, mostly posing as more of an expert than I really am. But the bottom line for me is that I need to find patients with tuberculosis in a place that facilitates my study of them. And Bolivia, along with Haiti, has case rates that are among the highest in the world. Certainly the highest in this hemisphere. I've been to Haiti as well, but things are so chaotic there that I prefer Bolivia. Not that Bolivia is not sometimes chaotic. There are good people to work with in Bolivia, and that's important. Good colleagues— good friends, good people. So I have gone back and worked there. Every couple of years or so, but usually only for about two weeks. I've even become pretty fluent in Spanish!"

I continued, "I tried hard not to be away from Susan and the kids when they were younger for more than a couple of weeks at a time. My family is important to me. I know scientists who have totally messed up their families as they pursued their research goals. Really, as they pursue what they perceive as fame. That's not me."

Before I could go further, Dave said to me, "I know about all that. You've done some research in Bolivia on methods for the rapid diagnosis of TB. I've read your papers, although some of the science stuff is pretty much beyond my ken. A couple of my younger CIA colleagues have looked at your stuff. They were impressed with your science and also with the way you tied decision analysis into interpreting your data. I really don't know what they—and you—were talking about. But I got the message that you are good at what you do."

"Well, thanks," I said. "I work hard and try to do good work. And some of the things I did, or started to do, on immune responses to TB in Bolivians living at different altitudes really interest me," I continued, "although I never completed enough of it to make much of a splash in the world of published papers. Those studies should have been finished—they were great studies—important stuff—but somehow they dropped between the cracks and never got finished up. Just ran out of time, I guess. Life gets busy, and it's easier to get funding for the laboratory work in Cleveland than for field studies in Bolivia."

"Okay," said my friend, "let me get down to the reasons I am here. It begins with Gonzalo Mamani. You know him, I believe."

"Yes, yes. My principal collaborator in Bolivia and good friend. A wonderful guy, really, and very smart."

"Tell me what you know about him."

"Well, he's a Bolivian doctor, Aymaran, in fact. Educated in Chile. Probably one of the best docs in Bolivia. He works at the Torax—Instituto de Torax—seeing patients with lung disease—there's a lot of it among Bolivian miners—and doing some high-altitude physiology research. How do people adapt to living their entire lives at altitudes where the air is so thin that their blood oxygen levels are low enough so that we here, in Cleveland, would prescribe oxygen for them? Interesting question. We did some studies together—not on that but on TB. In addition to those reported in the papers you say you read, we tried to figure out why TB case rates are so different among Bolivians living in high altitudes, the Altiplano, and at lower altitudes, near Santa Cruz. More than that, when the Bolivians who resettled from the La Paz area to the Yungas valleys northeast of the city—over the mountains down the eastern slopes to about 6,000 to 8,000 feet of altitude, they seem to have taken their susceptibility to TB with them. Except for those in one town, Suapi. Why should that be? And some of that work would still be going on if I could find the money to get back to Bolivia more often. I love Bolivia. I call it my *'segunda patria,'* my second homeland. And in Bolivia, Gonzalo is my best friend.

"Actually, Gonzalo is much more than a friend. A collaborator, a colleague, a fellow scientist. He spent a year with me in my lab here in 1977 and '78. One of my earliest post-docs. And one of the best. That's when and how I first came to know him. We worked well together then, and we've worked together a lot ever since."

Before Gonzalo Mamani spent that year in my laboratory, he had written to me from Bolivia saying he wished to learn research methods for the study of tuberculosis, which he noted was a major problem among his people. As I did with other applicants to my laboratory, I asked him to send me a letter in English and in his handwriting describing what he hoped to accomplish in a year with me. I had learned that professional letter writers were pretty facile at producing letters from applicants in the impoverished countries of the world. I was prepared to be sympathetic to such applicants, but they needed more than my sympathy to have productive experiences working with me.

Gonzalo was a handsome man, his features only moderately shaped by his Aymara ancestry. He was intelligent and a quick learner. His science knowledge acquired as a medical student in Chile was solid, especially so in chemistry, which was important in my laboratory. He caught on quickly and was facile with techniques requiring precision. Laboratory experiments, when successful, can be as heart-warming as rosy summer sunrises. When unsuccessful, when things go wrong, they can be tectonically frustrating. Icy winter nightfalls. Gonzalo handled both success and failure with a shrug and a smile. Additionally, he was outgoing and friendly with everyone he met. He fit well into the lab team. I could not have asked for a better post-doctoral fellow working with me, and we soon became close friends.

Our food arrived. Napkins in laps, we began eating. But slowly, as our conversation held our attentions.

"All right," Dave said. "Time to switch subjects. What do you know about lithium?"

"Lithium?"

"Yes, lithium."

"Well," I said, "I remember from high-school chemistry that it is a light metal. First in the periodic table column that includes sodium and potassium, I believe. Well, after hydrogen, I guess. Very reactive. I think I remember a chemistry teacher throwing a piece into water, and it caught fire. Or maybe I'm making that up. It was a long time ago. And I believe it is used in incendiary bombs. But this is not a part of chemistry that I know much about."

"Do you have a cell phone?" Dave asked.

"Yes." I reached into my jacket pocket.

"No, I don't need to see it. And a laptop computer?"

"Yeah."

"Those gadgets, plus lots of others, plus satellites and high-tech weapon systems depend on light-weight batteries. Those batteries are made with lithium. Without lithium, our modern world would grind to a halt. Without lithium, this country would stumble. Without lithium, our place at the table of international powers would be lost. Without lithium, America could not defend itself. And, of course, without lithium, you could not call your wife in Chicago to ask how the art affair is going."

"Okay," I said, wondering where this conversation was going.

"Lithium is a widespread element in the earth," Dave said. "However, lithium ore in lodes worth mining occurs in only three countries in the world."

"Let me guess," I interjected. "Bolivia is one of them."

"Right. And the others are China and North Korea." Dave shifted his weight in his chair and then continued, "These days my colleagues at the CIA think that China is the most important of all our potential adversaries, more so than North Korea. China is an emerging global power. We have frequent encounters with China that push the edge, sometimes with military aircraft, sometimes with computers and internet stuff, sometimes face-to-face with diplomats. We don't expect a war with China, but we surely want to be prepared for one. Even without war, if lithium could not be obtained from Bolivia, we would be beholden to China. Not a scenario those of us at the CIA look upon favorably."

"Wow! So Bolivia is important."

"Yes. Very much so."

Dave continued, "Evo Morales is Bolivia's new president."

"Yes, I know."

"Morales is a bit of an unknown for us. He's an indigenous, Aymara-speaking man with enormous popular support. He was elected after a series of rather ineffective presidents who came from the Bolivian military."

"Yes," I interjected. "The army is Bolivia's major political party."

"True. We in Washington assess Morales as a potential and lurking threat. Maybe that's unnecessarily pessimistic, but he is being bank-rolled by Chavez in Venezuela with his oil money, and he has allied himself with Castro in Cuba. So far, however, he has not been overtly anti-American. We pour lots of USAID money into Bolivia, and Morales does not want to lose that. You know," Dave continued, "Bolivia threw the Peace Corps out in 1971. That was under President Torres. That was dramatic and a great boost for Torres among Bolivia's leftists, but it didn't dampen the flow of American dollars into Bolivia and his pocket."

"I think I understand that," I said, "but I also think that Morales is less hostile to us than either Chavez or Castro. Or Torres, for that matter. Morales was elected, and the army stayed in its barracks rather than ousting him. In Bolivia that means something—a lot, actually—although I'm not quite sure what."

"You're right," Dave commented, "and we probably have little to fear at the moment. Morales depends on our dollars. But Bolivia has lots of natural gas, and if it can get pipelines completed to export natural gas to Argentina and Brazil, then the ball game may change. But let's put that aside, and get back to lithium."

"Okay." I picked up a piece of pita bread. We were eating slowly, as we were both focused on this conversation. The restaurant was not crowded, and it seemed to me that we might continue talking for some time. I flagged a waiter and ordered another round of drinks.

Dave continued, "Let's suppose we find ourselves in hostilities or merely in some sort of stand-off with China. Maybe over Korea. Maybe over the South China Sea. Whatever. The circumstances don't really matter. Then, Bolivia's lithium becomes critical to us. Bolivia would have us over the proverbial barrel. What might Evo Morales do then? This is an unwanted scenario that we at the CIA have struggled with."

"I can see that," I commented.

"And, I hope, you also see that we need every bit of inside information about Bolivia we can get," Dave commented. "Stuff that may not even seem to be important at the time, but that might turn out to be critical at some point."

"Yeah, I guess. I get that."

"So, we have spies in Bolivia. Most of them are based in our embassy in sham positions—titles such as 'cultural attaché.' The Bolivians know about them, of course. It's sort of a game. They have similar people in Washington, although not so many. However, we also have other spies, not out in the open, hopefully not known to Morales and his government."

"Real spy stuff," I interjected.

"Right. And one of them, perhaps the most important of them, is your Bolivian friend, Gonzalo Mamani."

I was surprised by this news, and uncertain how to respond. "Oh! Ah, okay, I guess."

"We believe," said Dave, "and Gonzalo believes, that his clandestine activities for us have become known to the Bolivian security folks. That is, in spy story-speak, 'his cover has been blown.' We must get him out of Bolivia, and soon. Like within a few days or maybe a week or two from now."

"Wow," was all I could say.

"Gonzalo agrees, and is ready to leave. However, and not surprisingly, he is scared. This is a big deal for him. It means leaving his homeland—forever. He's not married, so that's a little easier. But he is Bolivian, and his only experience out of South America is the year he spent with you in your laboratory. It won't be easy for him.

"Gonzalo doesn't think he would be allowed to board a flight to the U.S. He's right. He would certainly be arrested at the airport and wind up in a Bolivian jail. So he has to get out overland. Tough, but doable, we think, at least we hope. Gonzalo is ready to go, but he wants someone from our side to help. And the someone he wants is you!"

4

"HERE'S THE DEAL," Dave said as we started on the crème brulée we had each ordered. "Today is Monday. You fly to Bolivia Wednesday. Early morning flight to Miami, and then on to La Paz Wednesday night."

"Stop! Stop right now! I can't do that. My grant deadline is next week. If I miss that date, my lab is down the tubes. Two technician salaries, lab supplies and some minor equipment, sixty percent of my salary, and three years of research work depend on that NIH R01 and the 398 form I was working on when you walked into my office. This is my life. This is what I do for a living. This is me. My grant renewal is the most important thing in my life right now."

"Yes, we at the CIA know that," countered Dave. "And we are prepared to deal with your grant support in a way we think you will like. The CIA views successful extracting of Gonzalo as a national security issue, and for such matters all sorts of resources become available. Isn't your grant proposal pretty much finished?"

"Well, yes, but it needs polishing. The NIH funds only about one in ten proposals. I have a pretty good track record, but I cannot get complacent."

"What about animal and human rights protection assurances? Have those things been taken care of?" Dave asked. I was surprised that Dave knew this much about the grant submission process. I supposed he or someone had done a bit of homework.

"Yeah, they're all done. In fact, the proposal is pretty much ready to go. It and some forms need signatures, which I can get quickly. In fact, I suppose, Jennifer could walk it all through tomorrow." Somehow, part of my brain had begun to think that flying to La Paz on Wednesday night was unavoidable.

"This is really a pretty good restaurant," Dave commented. Why this digression? I had millions of thoughts and questions racing around inside my head. But Dave came back to the Bolivia junket. "We at the CIA are prepared to handle your grant renewal problem. Which institute funds your research?

"NIAID. Naional Institute of Allergy and Infectious Diseases."

"Okay. Send it to NIAID, as planned. Don't delay. It needs to get there this week, so FedEx it. Tomorrow."

"Sure, I could do that. I suppose, but it needs to be polished, checked, and rechecked. It must be as near to perfect as I can make it."

"Listen to me," Dave said. "Your proposal will be funded. It will be forwarded from NIAID to the Fogarty Center at the NIH. Fogarty does whatever it does for international research using whatever money it can find in the federal bureaucracy."

"Yes, I know," I commented. "I've been on a couple of their panels."

"Fogarty doesn't usually fund research, but they are ready to fund you using money given to them by the State Department specifically for that purpose. I'm not sure just how that will work, but there seems to be a way, and they will make it work—whoever 'they' are. Money will be shuffled around. Your award will not come from Fogarty but from NIAID, at least on paper, as a regular grant. And they will fund you for five years."

"Five years! But I have only proposed work for three. That's all the NIH does now."

"Five years. Provided, of course, that you agree to go to Bolivia and help rescue Gonzalo." Dave waved a credit card at the waiter.

I nodded and then shrugged my shoulders. "You've made it impossible for me to refuse."

"Not really, but you should know that Uncle Sam appreciates what you are about to undertake and is willing to reward you. Now, take me back to the Glidden House. Meet me there for breakfast at eight tomorrow morning. And bring your passport."

5

GLIDDEN HOUSE is a historic mansion located on the campus of Case Western Reserve University. It was built in 1909 by Francis Glidden, known as Frank, the scion of the founder of the Glidden Paint Company; and Glidden family members occupied it until 1953. At that time Western Reserve University (Case Institute of Technology would not join the university and add its name to it until years later) purchased it. Initially it housed the

Department of Psychology. In 1989 an addition enlarged it, and it became a B&B catering to university visitors.

I found Dave enjoying his breakfast. I picked up a cup of coffee and joined him. "Okay," I said. "There's lots you need to tell me about this proposed caper."

Dave pulled his briefcase up onto the table, opened it, and pulled out a manila envelope. "Here is your ticket to La Paz. American Airlines, business class. It's a long flight, and we want you to arrive relaxed and ready to take on the world. Well, at least Bolivia. And here's a membership pass to American airport lounges. You will have to wait all day in Miami for the night flight to Bolivia. Membership lounges are often pretty crowded these days, but the seats are better than in the terminal concourses. Get a snack. Have a drink, if you want. Hang onto the pass. Maybe you'll come home that way, I'm not sure.

"Next," Dave continued, "here is a MasterCard credit card. Limit is thirty thousand dollars, but you shouldn't need anything like that. You will need money, however. So here is a thousand dollars, all in fifties. That makes a wad, but bigger bills are hard to change. Next, I have for you two thousand Bolivian *bolivianos* and two thousand Peruvian *soles*, each worth about three hundred dollars. I hope you have a big money belt."

"I have a wallet that hangs down inside my pant leg. And I usually travel wearing a pair of those outdoor-type pants with lots of zippered pockets. I'm pretty savvy about hanging onto my money in places like Bolivia."

"Now," Dave said, "let me see your passport." I handed it to him, and he paged through it, examining each entry stamp. "You're okay," he said. "We don't want you caught with entry stamps that might raise eyebrows. Especially, no entry into Colombia, where the drug traffic is centered."

"No, I've never been to Colombia."

I took a look at my ticket to La Paz. "A one-way ticket," I commented. "How do I get home? And why the *soles*?"

"I don't know the answer to all of that. You'll find out in La Paz. And, of course, you have to get Gonzalo out, which will affect your return. I guess that if nothing else is offered, you can buy an airline ticket with that credit card. Once you are in Bolivia, you will be under the wing of the CIA folks there, not me."

I took the ticket and money, stuffing them into my jacket pockets. I hadn't really expected all of this, and had not brought my briefcase.

"You'll be getting a new passport with a new name," Dave said. "You should take passport photos with you. It'll make things easier. You should be able to find a kiosk in the Miami airport and get photos of yourself."

"Actually, the audio-visual guys at the med school will take passport photos. I can get them made this morning."

"Okay. Good."

"And some thoughts about what you should take," Dave added. "We want you to be viewed on arrival as a traveling businessman—and an important one. Do you have a dark blue suit?"

"Yes."

"Wear it flying down. But take along the multi-pocketed pants. You may need them as you make your way out with Gonzalo. Also, take along a small backpack as your carry-on."

"Okay. I have one. I can do that, although it seems to me not to fit with the suit."

"Well, just do it. And do not, do not, do not take a laptop or cell phone or any other electronic wizardry. You would probably have to abandon them, and we don't want the Bolivians to find them. Take your passport. Take a wallet—the MasterCard card I gave you, your driver's license, and the American airport lounge pass. Nothing else but money in it. No picture of Susan."

"Hey, this is beginning to sound like serious spy stuff," I said.

"Well, it is.

"As you know," Dave continued, "modern times have come to La Paz in recent years. You are booked into the Europa, a fairly new and modern hotel. You will need a couple of days to rest and adapt to the altitude."

"Yes, I know," I interjected. "I've been through *soroche* (acute altitude sickness) many times. I have Diamox at home and will take it, but it only ameliorates altitude adjustment somewhat. I don't usually get to do my altitude adaptation in such posh quarters, however."

"Good," added Dave. "You will arrive in La Paz early Thursday morning. By the time you clear immigration and customs, it will be about six A.M., I guess. Take a taxi down from the El Alto airport. Stay in your hotel. On Friday, be in the Bistro Bar there at six-thirty in the evening and order a pisco sour. Find a seat. Alone, in a corner. One of our people will find you.

"Good luck, and many thanks. I know this is sudden, but we have to move fast to get Gonzalo to safety. We mustn't let him wind up in a Bolivian *carcel.* I think that's the word for jail! And if we delay, he might. Now then, I have to get to the airport for a six-thirty flight to Washington National. How long will it take me in a taxi?"

"I'm picking up Susan at four-twenty-something. If you don't mind being a bit early, I'll collect you here at three-thirty and drive you out."

"Great. I'll be ready then."

"Meanwhile, if you have time on your hands. The Cleveland Museum of Art is just across the way. It's a good museum. There's a Warhol of Marilyn Monroe there that I really like. And some good impressionists, including one of Monet's water lilies. Good Asian art, but very little pre-Columbian Latin American."

On the way to the airport I had more questions for Dave. "What will happen to Gonzalo when... after... if... we get him out of Bolivia and safely to the U.S.?"

"Well, I guess he'll practice medicine. Maybe get a job in a hospital. Or open an office. What do MDs do to start out their lives in medicine?"

"Ahhh! You and your CIA friends haven't thought that through, I guess."

"Don't get testy. You're one of us now."

"Yeah, I guess. But if Gonzalo is going to continue in

medicine, he'll need to get a license in whatever state he settles in. That means he'll have to pass parts I and II of the National Board of Medical Examiners exam. Then he'll have to have one or, in most states, two years of supervised clinical training—internship, residency. And finally pass part III of the board exam."

"Won't his Chilean and Bolivian licenses count for anything?"

"Nope, not at all. But his degree from Chile will be accepted after he completes the required clinical training in an accredited U.S. hospital. I suggest you get him enrolled in a Kaplan cram course to study for the board exams as soon as he gets settled. Yes, he knows medicine, but those exams are tough and they include a lot of basic stuff that he hasn't dealt with since medical school. Maybe he could get an advanced medical clerkship or a clinical rotation in pulmonary disease while he is studying for the board exams. And of course, he'll need financial help, at least until he gets into an internship."

"Money will be no problem for him. We'll be sure of that."

"I guess you will. At least you should," I said.

"Suppose we settle him in Cleveland. Then you could help steer him through all of this."

I should have seen this coming, but somehow I had not. I really had no choice. "Okay, that makes some sense," I said. Provided, I thought to myself, that the escape from Bolivia comes off—for both of us.

"Another question," I continued. "How likely are the Bolivians to come after him? Here in the U.S., in Cleveland?"

"Not at all. Yes, they'll try—try hard—to catch him before he gets away, and they'll keep after him while he is on the run. And you too, of course. Then they could put him on trial as a spy. It would make Morales look like a patriotic hero. If they catch you, we can probably get you back here—you're an American citizen—although you'll probably have a few unpleasant months while we are negotiating. They'll have you all over the news. You know, 'Bolivia captures a spy from *Los Estados*.' However, as I said, Morales wants and needs our USAID money. Once Gonzalo is safely in the U.S., they'll give up, I think. To keep after him would mean admitting to weakness, and Morales depends too much on his *machismo* image to do that. And perhaps jeopardizing his USAID money." No part of this conversation was reassuring to me.

At the Cleveland airport I parked in the garage. Dave and I walked across the bridge to the terminal. "Once again, thanks," he said as he headed to check in, and I turned to go down to the baggage-claim area where I would meet Susan. "The CIA doesn't like to involve folks like you in its activities, but without your help we really can't get Gonzalo to safety."

If I can carry it off, I thought.

Susan arrived on time—actually about twenty minutes early. We met at carousel 6. "How was Chicago?" I asked as we waited for her bag.

"Great," she said. "And I had time to wander around the Institute of Art. One of the best art museums in the country, maybe the world, in my view. Marvelous collection of impressionists. And, to top it off, I connected with Nancy Ryan. We had dinner at the Cape Cod Room in the Drake."

"Terrific. Red snapper soup with sherry, I hope."

"Oh, yes, and a good crab entrée. So how have you been?"

Then I told her about Bolivia and Gonzalo.

JENNIFER ARRIVED in the lab shortly before ten on Tuesday morning. I asked her to come into my office and sit down.

"Sorry to be late," she said, "but that mongrel pooch of mine needed to go to the vet."

"No problem," I replied, "but there are things happening— out of control, maybe, really, in fact—that you need to know about. And I need your help."

"Sure. What can I do?"

I told her about Gonzalo and my urgent trip to Bolivia. And that I didn't know just what would be going on or just when I would be back. "I leave tomorrow morning. You'll have to keep things going in the lab while I'm away."

"That should be easy. We know what we are doing—at least at this point. But what about the grant renewal? It's due soon, isn't it? Right away, no?"

"Yeah, and you will have to pick up the IRB (Institutional Review Board) human rights and animal welfare stuff. It should be ready now. Then get the grant proposal FedExed out. This afternoon."

"Okay. I can do that if you print it out. You've been working on it a lot. Is it really ready to go?"

"Well, as ready as it's going to get." And I told her about the CIA funding and the Fogarty Center.

"Five years. Wow!"

"Yes, wow. You know, that's a bonanza. It really puts the squeeze on me to go and do this wild thing. Besides, I like Gonzalo, and I want to help him if I can."

"Will Gonzalo come back here?" she asked. "To the lab?"

"Well, I don't know. I guess not. I think not. He'll need to find a life for himself, and more time in this lab really won't help him."

"Okay, Boss. But if Gonzalo comes back to the lab, I'll have to leave."

"*What?*"

"Yeah. There's a lot goes on among the 'low life' that you and your kind don't realize."

"Low life?"

"You know, lab techs, post-docs, students. Worker bees. Sometimes we call ourselves the 'low life.'"

"Hey, I work in the lab too. I get my hands wet. Sometimes I even wash glassware!" I said.

"Yes, you do. But not too many—not most—of the principal investigators do."

"Okay. So I'm a good guy. Now, what's wrong with Gonzalo?"

"It's really not Gonzalo," she said. "It's Gonzalo and me. Well, yes, it is Gonzalo. When he was here back in '77 and '78 I had just started here. That was twenty years ago, and I was fresh out of college and pretty naïve about things. Although I thought I knew everything about everything, of course."

"I remember. I hired you just out of John Carroll University with a biochemistry major. And I remember you and Gonzalo working together. In fact," I mused, "I particularly recall one day you were cracking jokes as you set up to skin test guinea pigs."

"Yeah, that involved pulling numbered corks out of a box to establish random sequences for putting twelve skin tests on the flanks of each guinea pig. Somehow that seemed funny at the time."

"More than that," I commented, "you and he worked well together in the lab. He caught on quickly to some very tricky techniques. And to the precautions needed when working with virulent organisms."

"You know," she said, "he wouldn't let me work with the TB cultures. He said he was already infected with a positive skin test, so there was no risk for him."

"Actually," I interjected, "working in the hood with a UV light meant no risk for you—or anyone. Besides which, we rarely used virulent TB strains. Almost always we used the harmless H37Ra strain. I guess I can think of only a couple of times when we used possibly hazardous bugs, and I always did that work myself.

"You know," I continued, "you know as well as I do that most of what we do here is lab stuff—chemistry stuff—not TB bacteria and not guinea pigs."

"True."

"And Gonzalo seemed to me to catch on to that stuff quickly and become proficient. Of course, that was your doing mostly. It was you who taught him. It was my impression that you two worked well together. And that you became friends. Why your concerns now?"

"Right. Well, Gonzalo and I hit it off pretty well. In fact, pretty soon we started dating."

"I knew you got along," I said, "but I didn't know you were dating."

"Well, we were. And in about May, six weeks or so before Gonzalo would be returning to Bolivia, I found myself pregnant. Gonzalo was not really helpful or supportive. He suddenly was not the nice guy that we all thought he was. And that I thought I loved. He thought about himself, but not about me."

"Oh, wow," was all I could say.

"He and I discussed this, repeatedly, evening after evening. In the end, he proposed that he marry me and take me back to Bolivia with him. I couldn't bring myself to do that. I was not sure he really loved me. In fact, I think his love disappeared with my periods. Nor did I think I could be a Bolivian wife. I suggested that he marry me and stay here. But he wouldn't do that. Then he said I should get an abortion. In fact, I had thought of that, but I couldn't bring myself to do it. There was an unborn child growing in me. Could I kill it? No. So I began thinking of how I might disappear for nine months and then put the baby up for adoption. But I didn't like that either. It was to be my child. I didn't know how or what I was going to tell my parents."

"Oh, Jennifer," I said. "I had no idea that any of this was happening. If you'd have come to me I would have tried to help, although I'm not sure what I could have done."

"In the end, the problem took care of itself. I had a spontaneous miscarriage. But the whole experience was bad for me. It's probably why I'm still single. I have seen other guys, from time to time, but I just have not been able to get close to any man. And that's Gonzalo's fault, I believe. He behaved badly towards me. He is not—well, was not, anyway—a nice guy."

"Okay," I said. "Be that as it may, I leave tomorrow morning to help Gonzalo get out of Bolivia and back to the U.S. Where he will wind up, I don't know. It might be in Cleveland, I suppose, but it won't be in this lab. I promise you that. He'll need to establish a life for himself, presumably as a doctor, and more time here would not help with that. But if he drops in to visit, I'll welcome him."

"And if he drops in, I'll hide," said Jennifer. "He's just not an all-around nice guy."

"You know, Jennifer," I mused, "you paint an entirely different picture of Gonzalo than the one I have had in my mind. I guess most people are more complex than we sometimes realize. But in any case, I'm committed to help him. He was a good colleague—maybe the best post-doc fellow ever in the lab. And a wonderful friend to the family during the year we spent in Bolivia."

"And now he's a hero, a spy for America," Jennifer added.

"And wanted in Bolivia as a traitor."

PART III

LA PAZ, BOLIVIA, 1981

7

"WOW, LOOK AT that plane," enthused ten-year-old Eric, our youngest, as we waited to board the Braniff Airlines flight to La Paz. Braniff Airways had commissioned Alexander Calder to paint one of its four-engine, Douglas DC-8 jets, and we were about to begin our long-planned Bolivian saga on this colorful craft. "Flying Colors," Braniff had named it. We took our seats, Susan and fourteen-year-old daughter Alice on one side, Eric and I across the aisle. Window seats for the youngsters, although we hoped they would sleep during most of the long overnight flight.

It was Monday, July 6, and we had spent Sunday afternoon and night at a hotel near the Miami airport. After a morning flight from Cleveland to Miami, Eric and Alice had spent much of the day in the hotel pool. Meanwhile Susan and I rechecked and rechecked our baggage. What had we forgotten? Two years had gone into planning our soon-to-be-experienced sabbatical year in Bolivia. A grant from the Rockefeller Foundation together with funds husbanded from my Markle Scholars award had made this adventure possible.

I had much-dreamed-of research plans worked out in collaboration with Gonzalo Mamani, once a fellow in my laboratory, now my colleague and collaborator. The planned studies would be carried out at the Bolivian Instituto de Torax and the Facultad de Medicina of the Universidad Mayor de San Andrés in La Paz. Gonzalo and I had stayed in touch over the proposed studies. In fact, I had been to Bolivia for about ten days the preceding year, and Gonzalo and I had agreed on the general course of what we would do during my year in La Paz. Getting mail back and forth to work out protocols had frequently been frustrating, but

I trusted Gonzalo, and I had been encouraged by his responses to my letters.

I had jumped through the proper hoops for approval of human experimentation protocols in Cleveland. Gonzalo had obtained approval from the Bolivian Ministry of Health. More than that, he had organized a review board of Bolivian citizens to consider the rights of persons who would be studied. Approval of such a group was a necessary precursor to review in Cleveland. With that Bolivian approval in hand, the CWRU Institutional Review Board approval was relatively easy.

Lulled by the drone of jet engines, we managed some sleep. Early in the morning—very early—we stopped first in Guayaquil, Ecuador, followed by Lima, Peru. Then, with day breaking, up into and over the Andes Mountains. The Andes awed us. They rose steeply from the arid Pacific Coast. As we flew high above and over them, there were peaks on either side of us, the Cordillera Real to the east and the Cordillera Occidental to the west, with the high, flat Altiplano between. Beneath us, the blue water of Lake Titicaca soon appeared. We landed in La Paz and taxied to the small but modern terminal building.

We descended the stairs rolled up to the plane. We walked tentatively toward the terminal, uncertain where we should enter. There were neither signs nor persons to guide us, and we found ourselves standing with a group of confused passengers. Finally, a short Bolivian man wearing a uniform came from the terminal and herded us all to an inconspicuous doorway. Inside, we filled out a health form, presented our yellow fever vaccination cards, and cleared immigration and a cursory customs inspection. Gonzalo met us. Collecting ourselves and luggage into Gonzalo's elderly Volkswagen van, we headed out of the airport.

La Paz sits in a canyon, with the airport on the flat terrain above the city. The city was originally founded in 1548 in a canyon as a sheltered retreat for mule trains carrying silver and gold from the *cerro rico* (rich mountain) at Potosi to ocean-side ports for Spanish ships. El Alto (the height) is that part of the city above the canyon at an elevation of about 13,600 feet where the airport is located. As we reached the edge of El Alto and were about to descend the winding road to the city, I called to Gonzalo, "Stop!" There beneath us lay La Paz.

"Oh, look," said Alice, excitement in her voice. Beyond the city loomed the Andes, with Mount Illimani watching over the city. A rocky outcrop protruded through the mountain-capping glacier, creating an arrow pointing down to La Paz. That mountain with its arrow would become a favorite sight in our Bolivian year and become fixed in our memories of it.

Working with guide books in the Cleveland Heights library, Susan and I had identified a *pension*—boarding house—on Avenida Vente de Octubre. Gonzalo had checked it out and given it an okay. We settled in and asked for boiled water (which we treated with our iodine tablets, despite assurances that it had been boiled). Then we rested, as the stomach upset of acute mountain sickness—*soroche*—struck all of us. We rested, but could not sleep—another manifestation of *soroche*. We limited lunch and dinner to chicken soup; none of us were hungry.

With help from our genial host, I managed the *pension* telephone and called Gonzalo on Wednesday morning. He came by the *pension* and we greeted him warmly, now mostly recovered and somewhat adapted to the altitude. Gonzalo assured us that the four large cartons of household supplies, clothing, and personal effects that we had shipped to the Torax had arrived safely. He would deliver them to us in his venerable, hopefully immortal VW van as soon as we found a place to live. He offered to take us out to dinner, but we demurred until a later date when we would have more fully survived our *soroche*.

By afternoon of the following day we all felt much like ourselves. I ventured out and purchased a copy of *El Diario*, which Gonzalo and our *pension* hosts had told us contained the most real estate ads. Several calls from the wall-mounted telephone in the *pension* living area and several experiences with Bolivian buses resulted in identifying a furnished rental house that seemed suitable on Calle Cuatro (Fourth Street) in Obrajes, further down the canyon from the center of town and our *pension*. We all made the bus trip down, not wanting to impose on Gonzalo and knowing that we would soon have to master public transportation in La Paz. We liked the house, and agreed we could live there. We agreed to move in the following Monday. We had made it to Bolivia. We had found a place to live. Our year-long adventure was about to begin.

On Monday, July 13, we hired a taxi and moved from the pension to our new home in Obrajes. Gonzalo arrived in his venerable van with the goods we had sent ahead. Two trips for the four cartons. He also brought bottles of Paceña, a Bolivian beer, and of Inka Cola, a local soft drink—yellow with a licorice flavor. With his help, we mostly unpacked—at least our most urgent needs. Then a trip to a neighboring *tienda*, one of the nearly ubiquitous small shops that stock a little of almost everything, to pick up a few essentials and breakfast for the following day. We did our best, making our purchases in Spanish. Gonzalo, bemused but exercising restraint, stood by, occasionally nodding approval.

Our new home had its limitations. There was no central heating, and we had arrived in middle of an Andes mountain winter. There were in the house, however, two area heaters that used bottled propane gas. Fortunately replacements for the large and heavy canisters of propane were available in the local *tienda*.

"Hey," Alice called, "the bathroom faucets are labeled C and H, but the C isn't for cold; it's on the side where hot should be. And the H seems to be the cold one."

"Well," I said, "the Spanish word for hot is *caliente*—hot. And the H is left to go on the *frio* tap. Didn't you learn those words in your Spanish class?"

"It doesn't matter, anyway," added Eric. "Look. The pipes come together under the sink. It's all the same water."

In fact, we would spend the year without the luxury of a hot water heater. Water came to La Paz from a glacier-fed mountain river. There should have been plenty of it, but it was available only four hours a day. Our house, our home for a year, had a large water tank under the roof, so we would have water at all times. We were fortunate, Gonzalo told us. Our shower was equipped with an in-line heating element. A switch on the wall turned it on. The water temperature it achieved was variable and sometimes challenging. A high flow rate meant little time for heating, so lots of shower water was cold shower water. Alice, with her long blond hair, would manage but never like that arrangement.

There was a knock on the door. Susan opened it to greet a Bolivian woman. Obviously indigenous—probably Quechua, we would later judge. She was deeply tanned and had long, braided, black hair. She was short, probably no more than five feet. She wore a knitted alpaca poncho.

"Me llamo Maria. Quisiera volverme su empleada."

I translated for Susan: "Her name is Maria. She wants to work for us."

"Come in. Sit down," said Susan.

We learned that she lived with her daughter. She proposed to come to our house to work every day, but not on Sundays. She said she would prepare lunch and dinner for us and then leave for her evening meal with her daughter's family. She would bake bread every day. She would go each week with Susan to the market to buy food. She would help straighten up after meals and wash dishes, but she was a cook, not a housekeeper.

Gonzalo, who had been helping unpack boxes, came forward with important questions that we were too naïve to ask. "Have you worked for foreigners before? For Americans?"

"Si, Señor."

"Do you have references?"

Maria reached into a purse hung beneath her poncho and pulled out three folded letters from former employers. Two were from Americans, one from an English couple. All were positive, strongly so.

"Do you understand that Americans do not tolerate thievery? Not even of tiny items," Gonzalo asked.

"Si, claro, Señor."

Summoning up her not-yet-fluent Spanish, Susan asked Maria when she could start.

"Tomorrow. And I will take you to market in the morning. What time shall I arrive?"

"Nine o'clock," said Susan. "We will try you for two weeks.

Then, if all is satisfactory, you may continue. But if things are not going well in the first two weeks, you will have to leave."

"I understand," said Maria.

Maria would arrive promptly in the morning, and Susan would have her first experience shopping in the large central market of La Paz.

Our newly rented house looked out across the La Paz River. Across the valley spectacular red stone needles rose behind a few eucalyptus trees. The sight reminded Susan and me of Bryce Canyon in Utah, but on a smaller scale. And without the pine forests that surround Bryce; eucalyptus and sycamore trees are the only ones that survive at the above-tree-line altitude of La Paz.

That evening we enjoyed dinner with Gonzalo at a nearby *chifa*—a Chinese restaurant. Chinese food is the same all over the world, and it was an anchor point for Alice and Eric as they settled into life in La Paz. Later they would attend and make friends at the American Cooperative School.

We had arrived. We had made our initial altitude adjustment. We had found a place to live. We had connected with very helpful Gonzalo. We had hired Maria. Challenges and adjustments loomed, but we had no doubt that we would manage them. Life in Bolivia would be different from life in Cleveland Heights. Different, frequently surprising, sometimes challenging, always rewarding.

As dark descended into the valley of La Paz, Susan and I lay in bed, arms around each other, bodies together. "What do you think?" I whispered.

"I think this is great!"

8

"BUENOS DÍAS ¿CÓMO TE VA?" Gonzalo greeted me. "How are you?" It was Monday morning about 9:30. I had arrived at the Instituto de Torax, and I was ready to get started on the projects I had planned for my year of working with Gonzalo in Bolivia.

"Yes," I replied. *"Buenos días."* Then I added, "Thanks so much for helping us get moved in. I think the house in Obrajes will be perfect for us. And weren't we lucky to find Maria? Or for Maria to find us?"

"I think so," said Gonzalo. "Bolivia is a poor country, and there are lots of people seeking work.

"Now we have some important things to do this morning," Gonzalo continued.

"Good," I said. "Let's get to it. We need to make some specific plans."

"Hold on." American vernacular English came easily to Gonzalo after his year with me in Cleveland. "There are approvals we must get."

"I thought you had done that. I thought all of our protocols had been approved."

"Yes, they have been. But the important people have not met you. Until they meet you and approve of you, we cannot get started. You have to forget that you are an American. This is Bolivia. Personal contact means everything."

"Okay. So how do we go about this? And whom do I need to meet?"

"Well, you have to call on people. Courtesy calls, as much as anything. There should be no problems, but we must jump through the various hoops. Did you bring your CV?"

"Yes, I have three copies here with me, and also copies of my diplomas and board certification certificates."

"Good. If we need to, there's a kiosk down the street where we can get additional copies made. So let's start with the Director here at the Torax. Dr. Gomez. A fine man. You met him when you were here earlier. He asked about your arrival, and he wants to see you."

"Yes, I remember him. When can we see him? Do you think we can find him now?

"That should be no problem."

We had a pleasant chat over coffee with Dr. Gomez. I outlined our research plans. He had received copies of all of our protocols, which he might or might not have read. His English was marginal, so I tried to explain my ideas as best I could to someone who knew very little immunology. But he knew much about tuberculosis, and found my goals appropriate, if a bit ambitious, perhaps. He offered cooperation, and reassured us that the Torax radiology staff would be available to take chest films of those individuals for whom we might need them. He asked me to give a few lectures on tuberculosis to his staff and students during their rotations at the Torax. "Of course," I said.

I doubted that there was much about clinical tuberculosis that I could say to the staff at the Torax. They could teach me, I knew. As for the medical students, Gonzalo told me that junior students in the medical school had an entire semester focused on tuberculosis and other chest diseases. During that semester, they had three hours of lecture each week while spending the rest of their time on the wards of the Torax and the pulmonary services of the adjacent Hospital de Clinicas.

We then set off next to INLASA, the Instituto Nacional de Laboratorios de Salúd (National Institute of Health Laboratories). This institute housed the national tuberculosis reference microbiology laboratory. We planned to collaborate with the laboratory, and Gonzalo had enlisted Dra. Juliana Perez, INLASA's director, as a coinvestigator in our work. It would be important that the diagnosis of tuberculosis be confirmed by sputum smears and cultures. Juliana Perez was not only a competent bacteriologist but also an effective laboratory director. As with Dr. Gomez, I had met her—indeed had become friends with her—on an earlier trip to Bolivia. She was an attractive and intelligent woman. Her husband was an endocrinologist and one of Bolivia's most highly thought-of physicians. Her son was a medical student.

Some of our proposed studies would involve cell cultures. Maintaining sterility and careful technique were critical to success in such endeavors. Work of that sort had never been done in La Paz, but I was confident the facilities at INLASA were adequate for our studies.

We found Juliana Perez in the tuberculosis bacteriology laboratory hovered over a microscope, reviewing sputum smears with her technicians. This laboratory, which was devoted to the bacteriology of tuberculosis, was clearly the largest laboratory in the building. That so much space was devoted to tuberculosis reflected the realities of infectious disease in Bolivia. She walked toward us and greeted us warmly.

Juliana Perez was enthusiastic about collaborating with us. She introduced us to all of the technicians working in her laboratory. Some of them would be helping us with our upcoming studies. We spent an hour and a half with her, and I left feeling that the bacteriology part of our research efforts would be in good hands. More than that, I felt comfortable with the idea of introducing cell-culture work into that setting.

It was shortly after noon when we left INLASA. Gonzalo and I walked down the street and found a small restaurant. Later I would pack lunches before setting out in the morning, but our household was not yet ready for me to do that. I ordered two *salteñas* and a Coke. *Salteñas* are the Bolivian version of small meat pies that are *samosas* in East Africa and pasties in Michigan's Upper Peninsula. Gonzalo ordered the *menú*—the fixed-price meal. Like most Bolivians, he was accustomed to eating the largest meal of his day at midday.

After lunch we returned to Gonzalo's office. We next planned to visit the dean of the medical school—the Facultad de Medicina de la Universidad Mayor de San Andrés. He would surely not return from his noon meal until 2:00 or a bit later. We passed the time chatting, largely reminiscing about Gonzalo's year in Cleveland.

We set out walking through the large Hospital de Clínicas, the general hospital of La Paz, and then crossed Avenida Savedra to the nine-story medical school building. The dean's office was on the fourth floor; s sign at the door of the single elevator told us it was not working, so we walked up the stairs. An attractive young secretary put aside her nail file to ask our names and the purpose of our visit. Gonzalo replied to her in Spanish too rapid for me to follow. But I did understand that he was introducing me as an important professor visiting from the United States.

Soon we were seated in the office of Profesor Doctor Emanuel Rodrigo, the dean.

Gonzalo introduced me, and I presented copies of my CV, diplomas, and certificates. He glanced at them and added them to the large pile of papers on his desk. "We are honored to have a distinguished *'profesor catedratico'* here with us in La Paz," the dean told me. "I understand you will be spending a year with us."

"Yes," I said. "Dr. Mamani has been an outstanding collaborator and coinvestigator. I am fortunate to have been able to work with him in the past, and I look forward to continuing our collaboration. Also, the scientists I have met at the Torax and INLASA are exceptional persons. I look forward to working with them."

"Dr. Mamani has told me that you will be giving some lectures on tuberculosis at the Torax."

"Yes," I said. In fact Gonzalo and I had not had such discussions, although I expected it, and Dr. Gomez had made it clear that he wanted me to do so.

"And you lecture in Spanish?"

"As well as I can. And you can see for yourself that my Spanish is poor."

"Not at all. You speak very well. Certainly better than I could do in English." He shifted to English for that statement.

"You do not do yourself justice," I said. "I think you are more fluent than you credit yourself."

"Well now," the dean continued, "I understand you are an immunologist."

"Yes, of sorts, although my primary specialty is pulmonary disease. But my laboratory work has carried me into the field of immunology."

"Good. I want you to give a short course in immunology to our medical students. That field is sadly lacking from our curriculum. You should give a set of maybe six lectures. Teach our students the fundamentals of that important discipline. Our students need to know the science that underlies the pathology of diseases they will encounter and how that might affect the treatments they will offer."

"I can do that," I said. "I will need some time to prepare."

"This is July. You should start in September. My secretary will arrange the schedule."

Dean Rodrigo rose from his chair and offered his hand. Our meeting was over. After offering our thanks profusely, Gonzalo and I departed. "Well," said my friend, "that's a bit of good fortune. Your willingness to give a course—and the fact that he invited you to do so—have guaranteed us a free and clear path to carry out our studies."

"I'll need some help getting lectures into Spanish."

"No you won't. But if you do, I'll help."

We made our way down the stairs and out to the street. "That's it for today," Gonzalo said. "We have an appointment at the Ministry of Health tomorrow morning at ten. How about I pick you up about nine-fifteen? We should not be late."

"Fine."

"Can I drive you home?" Gonzalo offered.

"No. I think I'll walk."

"Are you sure you're up to it?"

"Yes, I'm fine," I replied.

"Okay, then. Tomorrow at nine-fifteen. No, make it nine o'clock."

"Good."

I turned and started down Avenida Savedra. Soon it wound its way steeply down to Obrajes. Trash lined the street. I walked past a wall upon which had been painted, *"No vote basura."* Well, I thought, that represents Bolivia in a couple of ways. *Votar* is the Spanish verb to vote. *Botar* the verb to discard or throw away. *Basura* is trash. In Spanish, as spoken in Bolivia, there is no distinction between the pronunciations of b and v. So this might have been a political statement or a futile attempt to keep *Paceños* from dumping trash.

I turned up Calle Cuatro and arrived home—our new home, our Bolivian home. I opened the door to be greeted by the aroma of freshly baked bread. "Hey, Dad," enthused Alice. "Maria baked bread. It's great. Have some. She made small loaves. '*Pancitos*,' she called them."

I took the bread Alice offered; it was delicious. Then I told Susan about my encounters of the day.

Over dinner I learned about the market trip led by Maria. Alice and Eric found it exciting. "We bargained all the time. And most of the *caseras*—vendors—that Maria knew gave us *ñapas*—extras," Alice reported. She was clearly pleased that she had learned two new words that had not been part of her Cleveland Heights Spanish lessons.

Susan had more to say about the market experience. "There was dirty water running in gutters, and the fruit and vegetable ladies were sprinkling it on their produce to keep it looking fresh. I've put what we bought into iodine water to soak, and we should carefully peel anything we don't cook. I bought some ground beef for hamburgers. It looks awfully lean. I might have to put fat in the pan to cook it! You know," she continued, "buying the meat was different. There was no bargaining over the price. However, Maria haggled and haggled about how many bones we had to take. Obviously, we don't want bones with hamburger. But they added to the weight, and we would pay by the pound—kilo, I guess. This is going to take some getting used to, but I'm sure we'll figure it out and that I will manage marketing."

"Yep, I'm sure you will."

Now adjusted to altitude, we all slept well that night. Altitude adjustment is a two-phase matter, I knew. The first part involves adjusting one's breathing so that one is no longer hyperventilating and getting rid of too much carbon dioxide. Blowing off carbon dioxide leads to changes in pH (acidity) in the body. One's tissues, especially the brain, tolerate that change poorly, and *soroche* results. That first phase of adjustment usually takes about thirty-six hours. The second aspect of adaptation to altitude involves increasing the oxygen-carrying capacity of one's red blood cells. Partly this is done by increasing their number. Additionally, changes in cell enzymes make red blood cells more efficient in carrying oxygen and transferring it to tissues. Those adjustments take a few weeks.

Gonzalo arrived in his van in the morning promptly at 9:00, and we headed up into town to the Ministry of Health. After warming a bench until about 10:30 we were ushered into the minister's office. He was a pleasant man, a physician, an obstetrician, an expert in neither public health nor any of the major health problems of Bolivia. Politically well connected, I supposed. But he seemed genuinely interested in the health problems of Bolivia, at least insofar as I could judge in this brief meeting. He sipped on a *mate de coca* from time to time. (A *mate* is a small pot typically containing an herbal tea.) Gonzalo reported to him on our meetings of the previous day. He nodded and then welcomed me to Bolivia. Fifteen minutes later we were again outside and walking to Gonzalo's van.

"You've passed," Gonzalo said. "We're all set. We can begin. Well, not quite. We have one more hurdle. We need to clear things with the military."

"Have you made contacts there?" I asked.

"Yes, but you need to get their approval. Our person there is Col. Alberto Surez. He's a good man, I think. He seems generally interested in the project. And he is well enough positioned to assure that everything will go smoothly for us."

"Okay, let's go."

The army's general headquarters—the *cuartel general*—was located just down the street from the medical center. We presented ourselves to the soldier stationed at the entrance and soon were ushered inside. We passed what looked like a World War II tank. "Bolivia's tank corps," Gonzalo said softly. Soon we were seated in the colonel's spacious attractively appointed office. We explained our proposed studies, repeating what Gonzalo had told the colonel earlier. He asked a few questions and then told us he would be glad to help in any way he could.

"At last we can begin," I told Gonzalo as we left.

"Right. And let's hope the work goes as smoothly as all these approvals did."

WHAT WERE THE STUDIES Gonzalo and I had planned and hoped to carry out during my year in Bolivia? They fell into two categories. First, I had ideas for simple, rapid tests for the diagnosis of tuberculosis—tests that could be carried out easily by minimally trained people and that would not require a laboratory. I thought we could find break-down products of tubercle bacilli in the urine of patients with TB. The amounts would be tiny—miniscule—but finding tiny amounts was one of the strengths of immunoassays. And immunoassays were what I was good at. If one could develop a urine test recognizing tuberculosis that was as reliable as a microscope-dependent sputum examination, it would greatly simplify the diagnosis and management of TB in remote areas such as those of Bolivia. And in many of these remote areas of Bolivia and similar remote areas in other parts of the world, tuberculosis was rampant.

Immunoassays can be done in a variety of ways. I thought I could set up one on a strip of paper-like cellulose acetate that could be dipped into urine. If the immunoassay found products of tubercle bacilli, a color would develop. Color, tuberculosis; no color, no tuberculosis.

Back in the Wearn Building I had put Jennifer to the task. She and I had made repeated experiments with the detection of small amounts of tubercle bacilli products, and had been pleased with our results. We had inoculated rabbits and mice, and we were pleased to have success with our assay in their urine. Going on from that, we had had success in testing the urine of four tuber-culosis patients in Cleveland and some healthy medical students. The time had come to take our assay to Bolivia.

Gonzalo and I planned to try out this test in Bolivian soldiers, and that would mean continuing to collaborate with Colonel Suarez. Employment for young men in Bolivia was hard to come by. Enlistment in the army was popular among Bolivian men after finishing secondary school. Health screening of recruits was cursory, and young men seeking to enlist were highly motivated not to disclose any symptoms of illness. Moreover, it is the nature of tuberculosis to have its peak incidence among young adults, especially so in high-prevalence areas.

We planned to try the simple test on a company of soldiers, and then bus them to the Torax for chest X-ray examinations to determine if they had tuberculosis. Based on what we knew of tuberculosis in Bolivia, we thought we would find many soldiers harboring TB—at least five percent, maybe ten percent. Gonzalo and I were enthusiastic about this study. We felt its results might be of considerable importance. We felt we could do this study quite easily with no more than an ordinary collection of unanticipated problems.

We planned to calculate predictive values—positive and negative—for our test. The sensitivity and specificity of diagnostic tests are often reported, and it is easy to calculate them. They are readily understood. But more useful information is presented when predictive values of tests are given. That sounds simple, but predictive values of tests vary with the prevalence of the disease in the population to which the test is applied. We would know how many of the soldiers we tested had tuberculosis because we would obtain X-ray examinations on all of them. Thus, we could calculate predictive values. How widely the results in soldiers could be applied to the general population of Bolivia was a matter that we could only speculate about.

The second group of studies we planned were more complex and less certain of outcome. They involved the study of tuberculosis in relation to altitude. Tuberculosis was common among people living on Bolivia's Altiplano and on the slopes of the Andes Mountains at altitudes of 14,000 to 16,000 feet. It was not common in the lowland eastern regions of the country. In addition to Bolivian Ministry of Health reports, in which we had limited confidence, there were data collected from 1967 to 1971 in association with an American Peace Corps tuberculosis control program in the Yungas. Elevations in the Yungas ranged from 4,000 to 8,000 feet. We were particularly interested in the town of Suapi at an elevation of about 5,000 feet. The Peace Corps data revealed less tuberculosis there than elsewhere in the Yungas, and TB skin testing results suggested to us that residents there might have some degree of immunity resulting from exposure to harmless environmental cousins of the tubercle bacillus, probably in the local soil.

We wanted to collect blood from persons living in Suapi and Coroico, a nearby town at about the same elevation with many cases of tuberculosis among its inhabitants. We would then harvest the immune cells from the blood we drew and stimulate them with antigens that Jennifer and I had harvested from tubercle bacilli and some of its soil-dwelling cousins. That, of course, meant getting the freshly drawn blood back to INLASA within a few hours. A challenge, but doable, Gonzalo and I thought. We would need to know the tuberculin skin test reactivity of the persons from whom we drew blood, and we would be looking for individuals ill with tuberculosis.

We would not only study cells from Coroico and Suapi. We would also study cells from individuals in La Paz, including the soldiers whom we screened for tuberculosis. In this manner—comparing Yungas results with soldiers in La Paz—we might get some clues about the effect of altitude with its low blood oxygen on cellular responses to tuberculosis antigens.

We expected to get all of this work under way within a week or two. That would prove to be somewhat optimistic.

10

LEAVING THE TORAX, we made our way up Avenida Save-dra. In La Paz, I had learned, directions are neither east or west nor left or right. In this canyon-side city they are up or down. We were headed up and across the mountains to the Yungas. Gonzalo was driving his van.

We passed the large stadium. *Paceños* (residents of La Paz) were proud of their *futbol* team. Helped by the need of competing teams from lower altitudes to adjust to the altitude and by the enhanced oxygen-carrying capacity of their own blood, *futbolistas* from La Paz did well in international competitions both at home in La Paz and elsewhere. Then we drove farther up through the district named Miraflores. Translated into English, Miraflores means something like "see the flowers." A vain hope in La Paz. No flowers and few trees grow at the altitude of La Paz. Sycamore trees lined the road in Miraflores, poled, however, as in Paris, where they are known as plane trees. They tolerate the altitude of La Paz.

Leaving the city, the road wound up in hairpin turns, following a tumbling river. This river would join that which flowed through La Paz—mostly under it, at least in the central city. Ultimately the water that cascaded beside us would make its way into the Amazon. As we climbed, trees became sparse, and sycamores gave way to eucalypti. Those trees, originally imported from Australia, thrived in the high, dry, Bolivian climate where others would not grow. Increasing amounts of snow bordered the road.

After an hour we reached the *cumbre* (summit). Gonzalo pulled his van off the road and stopped. A sign told us we were at 4,650 meters, about 15,260 feet, above sea level. We got out of the vehicle. The highest I had ever been with my feet on the ground. Gonzalo commented that another mountain road leaving La Paz climbed to about 17,000 feet, where the French had built a cosmic ray observation station. A Bolivian ski club had installed a primitive ski tow there at the edge of a glacier.

Overhead two Andean condors with their distinctive white heads soared, riding the mountain updrafts. These largest of raptors are found only high in the mountains of South America. Not far from us a herd of llamas and alpacas grazed. I knew about these camelids, the only large mammals indigenous to South America. Bolivians raise llamas as beasts of burden, although the loads they can carry are modest in size and weight. Bolivians also eat llama meat, although goat is preferred. Alpacas are never eaten; they are too valuable to be butchered.

The fleece of a llama is coarse with a long staple. Tough yarn. Good for rugs, and *bolsas* (sacks) but not for clothing. Alpacas, on the other hand, have soft fleece, yielding yarn much prized for hand-knit *chompas* (sweaters) and woven *ponchos*, and *aguayos*. An *aguayo* is a carrying cloth essential to every Andean woman. Square, about a yard wide, it is hand-woven in two parts that are then sewn together. A wide longitudinal area in each half, the *pampa* (field), is of a color specific to the region where its owner lives. Babies, groceries, items of value are folded into the *aguayo*, which is then carried on the woman's back, high, next to her shoulders, with corners coming together in front and held tenaciously in her hands.

Back in Gonzalo's van we were ready to make our way down into the Yungas. We drove back onto the road and began our descent on the Yungas road. It has been called "the world's most dangerous road." Hugging cliff sides, it was anything but an easy drive. Crosses, sometimes decorated with flowers, dotted the roadside at sharp drop-offs. Occasionally the remains of an irretrievable truck lay in the riverbed beneath the cross-marked roadside. As we rounded a curve where there was a steep drop-off we saw what appeared to be a family recovering possessions from a truck that had gone off the road and rested on its side in a stream below. *Derrumbes* (landslides) are frequent, and bulldozers work continuously at sites prone to these events.

In the 1930s Bolivia and neighboring Paraguay fought a war over a border region known as the Chaco. Dry and barren desert, the Chaco was thought to be rich in oil. A potential prize in an area the borders of which had never been clearly established, a potential prize claimed by both nations. It was a futile war that dragged on for about three years, ultimately ending in Paraguayan victory and ownership of about two-thirds of the disputed land. There was no oil in the Chaco, however. Many captives were taken on both sides. The Bolivians put their prisoners to work at road building, and we were about to descend the serpentine result of the labor of those men.

The name, Yungas, comes from the Aymara word, *yunka*,

variously said to mean warm place or place of trees. And warm and pleasant the Yungas is, with many trees. Lush vegetation, much of it appearing as though it had been created by Dr. Seuss. Flowers everywhere: hibiscus, bougainvillea, gardenias, and poinsettia bushes tall enough to stand under. The steep hillsides are terraced. Some fruit—avocados, papayas, oranges, and bananas—and coffee grow in the Yungas, but the major crop, the one that fills the carefully built and tended terraces, is coca. Coca leaves, looking somewhat like bay leaves, are picked from the low bushes three times a year. The leaves are dried on flagstone terraces. Crude cocaine is extracted with kerosene, which is then allowed to evaporate. The resulting proto-cocaine then makes its way north to be further refined before reaching Los Estados (the States).

The road before us swept across the face of a large cirque. Beneath us and ahead of us clouds shrouded much of the valley. Our destinations were Coroico and Suapi. First, however, we had to deal with Unduavi. The Yungas road divides at Unduavi into north and south branches. We would go north.

It was raining as we entered Unduavi; as we made repeated trips into the Yungas, we would come to believe that it never stopped raining in Unduavi. Moisture-laden prevailing winds from the southeast cross the continent and drop their water as they rise up the Andean slopes. In contrast to the dry desert western slopes of the Andes, the eastern mountain regions receive abundant rain. Trucks were parked along the roadside stretching back up the road. There was a toll station at Unduavi, and also a place to buy gasoline and diesel oil. It was primitive by North American gas station standards or those of gas stations in La Paz. One worked a handle to move gasoline into a glass chamber at the top of the pump. Compressing the handle on the gasoline pump's hose allowed the fuel to run down into the vehicle's gas tank. Thus we filled the tank of Gonzalo's van.

We entered the roadside building, and Gonzalo entered our names, vehicle make, and plate number, and our destination into a log book. "Do you suppose anyone will ever look at that entry?" I asked.

"No. But it's part of Bolivia's bureaucracy. Actually, someone will probably copy it out again and post it somewhere in La Paz. And no one will look at it there, either."

Driving on, we hugged the cliff side. Suddenly, rounding a curve, we found ourselves face-to-face, radiator grill-to-radiator grill, with an upward-bound truck. The truck was loaded with many *bolsas*—sacks of produce, we supposed. People sat on top of the truck's load. Cautiously, Gonzalo backed up until the road was wide enough for the truck to pass us. "Gonzalo," I said, "your van needs a loud air horn to warn approaching trucks. I'll pay for one for you."

"Yes," he replied, not continuing the conversation as he concentrated on the road.

We drove into Coroico. Not a large community, but a market town and a commercial center of sorts for the surrounding area. In Coroico we checked into the Hotel Prefectoral, Coroico's only hotel. We had our choice of rooms; there were no other guests.

Leaving Gonzalo's van at the hotel, we set off on foot to visit the local hospital. Bolivia had built small hospitals in five Yungas towns. Graduating medical students were required to spend their initial year after commencement at a rural clinic—an *año de provincias* (year in the provinces)—perhaps at one of those in the Yungas. It was hoped that some of these graduates would find medical practice in underserved communities attractive. In fact, the lack of supplies, support, and consultation opportunities and the rural living situations for former city-dwellers had the opposite effect. Few of them stayed beyond the obligatory year. None were present in Coroico at the time of our visit.

The Coroico hospital included a clinic area, a ward with four beds, and a small laboratory. It was staffed by two missionaries, Canadian nurses, who brought their skills and a small measure of Baptist evangelicism to Coroico. They provided the medical care available to the residents of Coroico. The laboratory was equipped to do urinalyses, sputum smears for tuberculosis, and assessment of anemia by a long-outmoded technique based on the color of blood in a finger stick. The nurses were interested in our proposed work, and we felt we could count on their support in this small community where news and opinions circulated widely at every morning market.

We next went in search of Martino Lopez, who we had learned was the *alcalde* (mayor). We found him in a bar and treated him to another *cerveza* (beer), also getting beer for ourselves. We explained that we would make many trips to Coroico and Suapi, depending on how our work went. Each time we would want to draw one syringe-full sample of blood from an individual with tuberculosis—the Canadian nurses had offered to help identify those persons—and also from one healthy individual of about the same age. We would pay our subjects thirty *bolivianos* for each blood drawing. Mayor Lopez offered his support—and ordered another round of beer for the three of us. In fact, he would be pleased if we would take his blood for *estas investigaciónes muy importantes* (these very important studies). I paid the bar bill for the three of us, and Gonzalo and I headed back to the hotel for dinner.

The menu at the dining room in the Hotel Prefectoral offered two entrées: *lomo montado* and *Milanesa*. Gonzalo chose the *lomo* (loin, steak). I chose the *Milanesa*, something Italian, I presumed. Gonzalo's *lomo* arrived with a fried egg on top of it—the *montado* part of it, I supposed. My *Milanesa* was, I assumed, intended to be a cutlet in an Italian style. At least it appeared to have spaghetti sauce on it. The two pieces of meat looked identical. Goat, per-haps. We had seen many goats as we drove into town. No cattle. Rice and fried plantain banana slices accompanied the meal. The *postre* (dessert) was a flan that was delicious. The best part of the meal.

A beautiful morning dawned in Coroico. We turned Gon-zalo's van onto the road to Suapi, a road better suited to mules than to automotive vehicles. After fording three small rivers we mounted a ridge and saw Suapi nestled in the valley beyond us. We drove down and into the central plaza. Suapi was too small a town to have an *alcalde*, but *Alcalde* Lopez in Coroico had given us the name of a man who he assured us was the *de facto* leader of the town. A crowd gathered, and Gonzalo's van was inspected and much admired despite its obvious age. When we identified ourselves as *médicos*, a young woman was brought to us. She opened her shirt to reveal a red and angry left breast, clearly infected. A cellulitis, Gonzalo and I agreed. "Is there a *farmacia* (pharmacy) in Suapi?" Gonzalo asked.

"Si, Señor," said a man who was obviously the town leader Lopez had identified.

We led the woman to the pharmacy. Gonzalo purchased a syringe-full of penicillin, which he injected into her shoulder. I then purchased a ten-day supply of oral penicillin. "Take these tablets twice a day until they are all gone," directed Gonzalo. "Even after your breast is better, keep taking them."

"Gracias, muchisimas gracias." The woman took the penicillin and smiled.

With such a propitious entry, we found our proposal to draw blood in Suapi received graciously. The proffered thirty *boliviano* payment would be welcome in this small village.

We headed back to La Paz, planning to time our return driving time, back to Coroico and then over the *cumbre* to La Paz. Approximately fifty miles. Five hours, we estimated, but it would take longer on this trip. As we traversed the large cirque above Unduavi, Gonzalo's van sputtered, then came to a stop. "Shit," Gonzalo said. "We're out of gas!"

"We passed a *'Se Vende Gasolina'* sign back a bit," I said.

"Too far to walk, I think," Gonzalo replied. "Get out and give me a shove. If I can roll back to the last curve, we can turn around and coast downhill, hopefully as far as the gas place you saw."

We managed the turn and, with an occasional further shove by me, we rolled down through three switchbacks to the small building where I had seen gasoline for sale. In response to our query, a boy whom I judged to be about ten or twelve years old indicated that he had gasoline that he could sell to us. He put the end of a length of hose into a large drum and sucked on it to draw gasoline into it. After spitting out gasoline from his mouth, he put the end of the hose into a metal pitcher on the ground. Gasoline drained into the pitcher. "Two gallons," a painted label on the container said. I wondered what that meant to a Bolivian boy who probably had been schooled in liters, if at all. We asked for five pitchers of fuel. He repeated the siphoning of fuel four additional times. With a funnel in the van's gas port, the boy poured each of the five pitchers of gasoline into the van's tank. We paid the boy and were soon back on the road to La Paz.

Our plan for our studies in the Yungas was to drive to Coroico, identify our donors, get up early the next morning and collect our blood samples. We would then drive to Suapi and collect blood there before heading back to La Paz. One of Juliana Perez's laboratory technicians would wait at INLASA for us, ready to work into the evening to help us process our samples. The cell culture studies we wanted to carry out at INLASA required viable cells, and that meant getting them separated from the blood and into appropriate culture media without delay. We could not run out of gas again. "We'll have to be sure to fill the van's tank in Coroico every time," I said to Gonzalo.

"Right, for sure."

As the year progressed, our work went as smoothly as one might expect. The studies in Bolivian army recruits were done easily, and the results were encouraging. We were grateful to Colonel Suarez, who made arrangements for us and facilitated the work. Our results were about as we anticipated. Our rapid test worked well. And we found a goodly number of Bolivian soldiers with tuberculosis who were thus able to be treated.

The Yungas studies were less consistently productive. The cell studies gave variable results. Perhaps, we thought, because the cells were less viable than we had hoped they would be after the long hours of transport. In any event, variable results mandated larger numbers of individual experiments, and my sabbatical year ran its course before we could accomplish that. Be that as it may have been and accepting that most medical research has limitations imposed by circumstances, Gonzalo and I were satisfied with our year-long effort.

My medical school lectures were well received, I thought,

and my Spanish fluency improved. In fact, my medical Spanish vocabulary rapidly expanded to meet the challenges of lecturing in that language. But there were interruptions when classes were cancelled, some for holidays, some for reasons I did not understand. One day I arrived at the medical school to find the place shut down and locked tight. I found a janitor and asked, "Is the medical school closed?"

"Of course. Pelé is here from Brazil playing *futbol* in the stadium."

11

ONE DAY GONZALO suggested to me that I come with him to see two of his patients at their homes. "The first is a man with silicosis. He is terribly short of breath, so I try to visit him in his home," Gonzalo said. "He has bad, really advanced silicosis from working in the mines."

"Don't miners wear masks, respirators?" I asked.

"Well, yes, maybe. They are supposed to be supplied with effective respirators, but they are usually given simple cloth masks that won't keep out the very small dust particles that do the damage. And real respirators are uncomfortable and hot, so the miners don't want them. And back when this man was in the mines, nothing was done to protect them.

"My patient lives up in El Alto, so we'll drive up there."

"What are they mining? What was he mining?" I asked.

"Well, gold, silver. The *cerro rico* at Potosi is still yielding valuable minerals. That's where my patient worked. He can no longer work, so now he lives with his daughter in El Alto."

We found the man sitting on a stool outside his modest home. He was leaning forward, his elbows on his knees in a position that optimized his respiration while minimizing the effort he needed to make. As we approached, a young woman—his daughter, I presumed—came to greet us. A young girl, perhaps three years old, I thought, clung to her. "He's doing pretty well," she said to Gonzalo. "Nothing has changed. He uses the inhaler you gave him, but it doesn't seem to help him much."

"No," Gonzalo said to her. "There is really nothing much we can do for him. You are a kind and generous person to take care of him."

"He's my father."

Gonzalo took out his stethoscope and listened to his patient's chest. He also felt his pulse, took his blood pressure, and listened to his heart. He looked carefully at his fingernails to judge how pink—how well oxygenated—they were.

"You are doing pretty well, my friend," Gonzalo said to his patient. "Just don't try to do too much. Don't chase too many pretty *chicas*."

His patient smiled. "No, I let the the girls chase me."

"Step inside," his daughter said. "I'll get money to pay you."

In the small room there was an open-topped cardboard box with two guinea pigs in it. *"Cobayos,"* I said. "Pets?"

"No," she smiled. "Dinner tonight. We call them *cuis*, for the sound they make." Turning to Gonzalo she asked, "How much do I owe you? Did I pay you last time?"

"Five *bolivianos*. Yes, you did pay me before." The young woman took coins from a small purse and gave them to Gonzalo.

"Your husband is not here today," Gonzalo commented.

"No, he went down to La Paz. He heard they are working on paving some roads. He hopes he might find some work there."

As we drove back to the city, I said to Gonzalo, "Five *bolivianos*! I would guess the gasoline you used to make this visit cost more than that."

"Well, he and his daughter's family have almost nothing. Times are hard. Times in Bolivia are always hard, I guess. But now we are going to see a patient who lives in Calacoto and is rich. I can charge her more. And," he added, "the family wants you, the famous professor, to see her."

"Okay, I guess, but I doubt that I could add much."

"She has metastatic cancer. Ovarian. She won't live much longer. She's a courageous woman. It's her family members that are the problem. Two daughters and a son. The daughters are okay, but the son insists that I cure her. Ridiculous."

We arrived at a large house on a substantial lot. Obviously the home of wealthy people. A maid ushered us into the living room, where a bed had been set up for the dowager. The son and two daughters were present, the daughters sitting in arm chairs, the son restless, pacing, clearly uncomfortable with the situation. He introduced us to two Bolivian doctors who were present. Gonzalo greeted them—colleagues, whom he knew—and introduced me. One of them had a flask of the patient's urine and was holding it up to light at a window so that he could examine it. To what medical purpose, I could not imagine. Probably to impress the family, I supposed.

I sat on the edge of the patient's bed and introduced myself. "I am an American doctor," I said. "Your family and Doctor Mamani asked me to see you."

"Yes. Thank you for coming."

"You have cancer."

"I know that—from one of my ovaries. And I know that I am dying. You cannot change that. And I do not expect you to do so."

"Are you comfortable?" I asked. "Have you pain?"

"Yes, no. They have given me morphine. I am comfortable. No pain. But I sleep a lot. I am ready to die. It will happen soon, I think."

I pulled down her sheet and felt her abdomen. It was rock hard, obviously full of tumor.

"Doctor," she said softly, "I am glad my family is here. I thank you for coming to see me. Now it is time for you and the other doctors to leave. I am ready to die, and I want to die in peace."

I pulled up the sheet to cover her. "You are a brave woman. I wish you comfort and peace."

I rose and walked across the room. Gonzalo, the woman's son, and the two Bolivian doctors joined me. "What is your opinion?" asked the son.

"She has cancer. You know that; she knows that. There is

nothing more that can be done for her. You, all of you, also know that, and she knows that. She is glad that her family is here, and she wants to be left alone to die in peace. I suggest that all of us—we *médicos*—leave her alone with her family. That's what she wants. And there is nothing our presence here can do to help her."

"But we want to be sure that she gets the best medical care possible," said her son.

"The best medical care she can get at this point is peace and quiet. We should all of us leave."

"Is there nothing more you can do?" once again asked the son.

"What we, and especially you, can do is allow her to die with dignity and peace. Our presence here does nothing to add to that. In fact, it makes the situation worse for her. She is ready to die and wants to do so with dignity. My colleagues," I said turning toward Gonzalo and the two Bolivian doctors, "it is time for us to depart and leave this courageous woman and her family in the hands of God."

Back in Gonzalo's van he said to me, "Thank you. I could not have said what you said. Those two doctors are simply after her money. They will send huge bills."

"And you, what will you charge?"

"Five *bolivianos*, I think."

12

IT WAS SUNDAY MORNING. A beautiful, sunny morning. We were looking forward to an expedition with Gonzalo when he arrived at our door.

"Where are you going to take us today?" Susan asked as she greeted him with a smile and a hug.

"No place, today, and I can't stay long. There's a *golpe* going on."

"*Golpe?*"

"Yes, a *golpe del estado*. A *coup d'état*. Or at least an attempt at one. No one can tell whether it will succeed. You'll have to stay home. And depending on how it goes, there may be a curfew, a *toca de queda*. I'll tell you what I know. But first, get some money. We need to go to the *tienda*. You need to buy what you can to survive for three or four days without going outside. No marketing tomorrow. All the markets will be closed anyway. Maria won't come, I am sure."

With Gonzalo we hustled to the neighboring *tienda*. There was a line at the counter and people were stripping the shelves of everything that looked edible. Susan and Alice joined in the scramble, while Eric, Gonzalo, and I waited outside.

Back in the house, Gonzalo reported to us, "I really only know what I heard on the radio this morning. And what I know that always happens with *golpes*. We have them fairly often, which is bad. Bad for Bolivia. Bolivia's president is an army general. An air force general wants to throw him out and take over. What will happen? No one knows, but it may be several days before one of them wins and things settle back down. I guess this is our political system. It's terrible. Terrible for Bolivia.

"You'll mostly have to make do with what you now have in the house. There is a *chifa* (Chinese restaurant) around the corner. If anything stays open, it will. You may be able to eat there, but go early. You must be home and in the house before it gets dark. It is unlikely that there will be any fighting here in Obrajes, but you can never tell. Bolivian soldiers loyal to one contender or the other will be shooting at each other. What a shame!"

As Gonzalo was leaving, an airplane flew over us. We were below but not far from the army headquarters. The air force was now attacking, flexing its muscles, I supposed. The aircraft appeared to be bombing the army buildings, but as it passed overhead it continued to release its load. "Look," Eric commented, "it's not dropping bombs. It's dropping garbage!"

"No surprise," Gonzalo commented. "No one should be hurt. That would be upsetting. Bolivia's tank, by the way, is now out and parked on the Prado in front of the university. The students should know that the military wants them to stay in their dormitories, regardless of who wins. *Asi es Bolivia.*"

Life settled down and boredom settled in. We had all come to love Bolivia and found it exciting. Whatever exciting things were going on elsewhere, however, they did not reach our house on Calle Cuatro. We played bridge and rummy, but card games soon lost their appeal.

Three days later Gonzalo returned. "It's over. The army won. The air force general's son, a pilot, crashed his plane doing stunts over Lake Titicaca. He was killed. Now we have a national day of mourning, declared by the army general, who has kept his seat as president."

Only in Bolivia, I thought. Only in this crazy country I had come to love.

13

"THERE'S SOMETHING going on at the university," Susan said at dinner one Monday evening. "Maria and I were on the bus with our baskets of groceries when we passed the university. You know, the building up there on the lower end of the Prado."

"Yes, I know that building. It's the main university building. But not the medical school," I said.

"Well, today there are all sorts of banners with slogans hanging out the windows. Maria said she has heard that the students have taken over."

"My guess would be not all of the students," I commented. "Just an activist group. Perhaps left wing—or perhaps right wing."

"What do you suppose they want?"

"Who knows? Not lower tuition; the university is free. So is board. They charge for food in the cafeteria, I think. Maybe they want that free too. Or maybe there's a professor they don't like."

"The university is free?" Alice asked. "Don't they have to pay tuition?"

"Nope. You know, anyone who finishes high school can enter

the university. At the medical school there are about a thousand students in the first-year class. There's no entrance exam. Finish high school and you're ready to learn to be a doctor. It's the European system. No undergraduate degree before medical school, but a longer medical school course."

"A thousand of them in the first year!"

"More or less. No entrance exam, but at the end of the first year there is a tough exam that they have to pass to move on. So there are only about two hundred second-year students."

"What happens if they flunk the first-year exam?"

"Well, they're out, but not really. They can sign up and repeat the first year again—as many times as they want. And remember, free room and board!

"This short immunology course I've been teaching. Right at the start a student asked if I would be taking attendance. Another asked if there would be an exam. I told them that I thought what I would be telling them about should interest them and might be important as they learned more clinical medicine. But the learning was up to them. No attendance taking, no exam. I think that sort of surprised them all. Anyway, most of them have stuck with it."

Susan brought the conversation back to the happenings at the university building that she had passed on the bus. "There is a big banner with a picture of a bearded man. Who would that be?"

"Che Guevara, I would guess."

"Who is Che Guevara?" Alice asked.

"Well," I said, "he was a Bolivian revolutionary who became a big-time folk hero. He went to Cuba at one point and linked up with Fidel Castro there. In Bolivia, he traveled widely in rural areas and urged *campesinos* to join his revolution. Although he was revered by leftist students, he got nowhere with Bolivian farmers. What he urged them to do was to follow him in his battle against land holders. He would redistribute land so that small farmers owned their own farms, the land they worked."

"The *campesinos* must have liked that," Alice commented.

"No, they didn't. What Che seemed not to know was that all the big land holdings had been broken up a couple of decades earlier. The small farmers whom he wanted to enlist in his revolution already owned their *fincas*."

"Pretty stupid," commented Eric. "What happened?"

"So," I continued, "the Bolivian government—the army, especially—wanted to get rid of him, but he was moving from place to place, hiding. They put a price on his head. They offered a reward to anyone that could tell them where he was.

"Che was fairly well hidden in a farm house in a rural area— not the Yungas, but a place like it. One day a car drove up. A man got out, entered the house, and shot Guevara. Who did it? Did someone collect the reward? No one knows. Or if they do, they're not telling. That was in 1969, but he is still remembered by Bolivia's leftists."

"Well," said Susan, "Che may be dead, but there still are students who want to start a revolution. And they have not only seized the university building, but they have also torn up the paving stones on the road at the side of the university. The vehicle entrance is blocked."

Alice and Eric had stopped eating and were listening wide-eyed to their mother. "Yes, kids," I said to them. "Democracy and free speech are precious. They're not always easy to come by in Bolivia. But this business by the students is stupid and likely to get them nothing—except maybe hurt."

"The bus was stopped at the traffic light there," Susan continued. "There were soldiers on the sidewalk, across the street from the university, just in front of where the bus was stopped. One of them raised his rifle and fired at the university. I don't know whether he wanted to shoot a student, and I really couldn't see what he hit. But I think just a part of the building wall."

Susan continued her account. "Maria said that the soldiers will turn off the electricity and water to the building. Then just wait."

"You know," I said, "that's smart. No ugly confrontation. No battle. Nobody hurt. Nothing to lose, as far as the army goes."

"How long will this go on?" Alice asked.

"Well, that's hard to say."

"Until they can no longer tolerate unflushed toilets, maybe," Eric guessed.

"Yep. It's going to get mighty unpleasant for the students holed up in there."

"So in the end, the students will simply have to give up?" Alice asked.

"I guess so. And I also guess that this is not the first time something like this has happened."

"What will happen to them, the students?" Alice continued.

"Oh, nothing, I suppose. This is Bolivia."

"But in the U.S., something like this would get them expelled. And arrested, probably."

"Yes," I said, "but this is Bolivia."

14

THE BUS CLIMBED UP from Obrajes toward the center of La Paz. We passed an army post with a placard announcing, "ANTOFAGASTA ES Y SERA BOLIVIANA" (Antofagasta is and will be Bolivian). Antofagasta had been Bolivia's seaport. Seeking greater access to the rich deposits of guano in bird rookeries on the Pacific Coast, Bolivia had invaded Chile and seized some of the coastal territory. Chile and Peru had responded to this attack, defeated the Bolivians, and annexed Antofagasta and the neighboring costal region. Bolivia was left without access to the sea, left with no easy way to export its many mineral treasures.

The bus continued up the main thoroughfare, which changed its name from 6 de Agosto (August 6) to 16 de Julio (July 16), thus commemorating two Bolivian holidays. We left the bus at the cathedral. Alice and Eric were awed at the large sanctuary. The altar impressed them, as did several side chapels. Susan and I had seen other cathedrals and were less awed.

Calle Sagarnaga (Sagarnaga Street) climbed up beside the cathedral. It housed many small shops. Along the street, vendors—women for the most part—displayed their wares, with goods spread on their *aguayos*. "Why do all the women selling oranges sit together?" wondered Alice. "Wouldn't each want her special place?" Many vendors offered coca leaves. At one corner a woman was selling dried llama fetuses. She had a moist coca leaf on her forehead. She told us that it was important to bury a llama fetus beneath the main room of every new *casita* (small or special house). Otherwise misfortune would stalk the house.

"Do you suppose we have a buried llama?" Eric asked.

We browsed, wandering into and out of several shops. Susan was intrigued with the artisanal handcrafts for sale, especially the textiles. She purchased a beautifully embroidered *pechero* (small item of clothing that hangs like a bib) and a fine *aguayo*. Eric found an *honda* (sling) and Alice a pair of *aretes* (earrings). Then back by bus to dinner at our Obrajes home.

One Sunday morning Gonzalo picked us up in his VW van. Susan had packed a picnic lunch, and we were headed for the Valle de la Luna (Valley of the Moon). We drove downhill from Obrajes to Calacoto. There, at a lower altitude, trees and flowers grew. Wealthy *Paceños* lived there, as did American embassy personnel. Further down, the road flattened out, and a side road took off to the right. We turned and drove past a brick yard, then up again, and into an area that could have been mistaken for the canyons of Utah. Water had carved and shaped sandstone into a sculpture garden. We enjoyed the lunch Susan had packed. She had picked up "broasted chicken"—"Whatever that means," she commented—from a street corner vendor. Whatever it was, we all thought it special and delicious. We were soon licking our fingers.

Alice and Eric began climbing and jumping on rock walls. "Take it easy, kids," I admonished. "No broken bones, please." We walked along the trail, sometimes as wide as a road, sometimes cut narrowly between towering rock walls. It was a fun outing, we all agreed.

"Where shall I take you next Sunday?" Gonzalo asked. Sunday outings with Gonzalo had become frequent. He seemed to enjoy these opportunities to show us his country.

"How about an Inca road?" Alice said.

"Yes. Great idea."

And so the following Sunday found us driving up the Palca road. We were awed by the views of Mount Mururata, inured to the unremitting and spectacular Andean mountain scenery as we had become. We reached the road to the Mina San Francisco (St. Francis Mine) and turned to climb it. This rugged and unpaved road survived because it gave access to a wolfram (tungsten ore) mine and hence was heavily traveled by trucks. But on this Sunday we met no traffic; we met only llamas tended by *campesinos*. Across the narrow valley, paralleling us, was the obvious line of an earlier highway, no longer in use, undoubtedly the route of the Inca road we hoped to encounter.

At the head of the valley, we found ourselves at the base of a large cirque, looking at the garden wall between the peaks of Mt. Taquesi to the north and Mt. Mururata to the south. We forded the river and left Gonzalo's van near a mine service building. A few yards ahead the track from the other side of the valley curved to approach us, and then doubled back to begin its climb up the mountain ridge. Vegetation was limited to clumps of a stiff, coarse grass.

Taking our lunch with us, we began our ascent on foot, following the broad Inca road. It maintained a breadth of anywhere from about six to about twenty feet. The grade was uniform, the course straight between switchbacks. Shortly we came upon remnants of paving: large fitted stones arranged radially on switchbacks, oblique drainage troughs paved in stone, and well-built stone retaining walls. Time and lack of maintenance had covered most of the surface with dirt and allowed many of the metaling stones to work their way down the mountainside.

About two thirds of the way up, the road entered a narrow cut with massive granite walls on either side. Here the Inca road was preserved in what we judged to be close to its original condition. The grade was steep, and the road had been laid in sloping steps, each rising about six to eight inches, each step six to eight feet deep. We stopped, rested, and spread out the lunch Susan had packed.

After lunch we continued our climb to the summit. A crude wooden cross was set in a rough cairn. A llama train with two herders rounded a corner and passed us by. The Inca-built road was still in use. We would long remember this unique outing with its glimpses into Andean history.

15

IN AUGUST WE CELEBRATED our wedding anniversary. We went out to dinner at a restaurant at the top of the tallest building in La Paz. The restaurant was named Las Estrellas. From Spanish, *Las Estrellas* translates to "The Stars." What else would one name the only roof-top restaurant in La Paz?

October brought Alice's fifteenth birthday, an event of great importance in Latin American cultures, the advent of woman-hood, an occasion for a celebration. Gonzalo offered a trip to Lake Titicaca, to which Alice responded with enthusiasm. At the lake, Gonzalo parked his well-traveled van beside the house of a Señor Quispe, whom he knew and had treated for asthma. Señor Quispe had a launch, and Gonzalo negotiated with him for a trip to the island of Suriqui. As we crossed to the island, we passed two reed boats, *balsas de totora*, from which men were casting nets. On the island we found men busily constructing reed boats. One of them, who seemed to be in charge, disappeared into his house and reappeared with a collection of papers. Letters, airplane brochures, maps. He was one of the Bolivian artisans whom Thor Heyerdahl had taken to Morocco to build the *Ra II*, the reed boat that successfully crossed the Atlantic.

On another memorable trip across the Altiplano to the region of Lake Titicaca, Gonzalo took us to Tiahuanacu, a large pre-Inca site with a centrally located, massive, monolithic figure, presum-ably of a deity. People of the early indigenous cultures worshiped Pacha Mama, the earth mother, and Inti, the son god, Gonzalo told us. The monolith presumably represented Inti. At Tiahua-nacu we also saw a stone gate or arch with a carved lintel, and a sunken area surrounded by walls adorned with carved faces. Yet to be much studied by archeologists, Tiahuanacu was both fascinating and puzzling.

On a Saturday evening, Gonzalo took us to a *peña*. Tucked behind a shop off Calle Sagarnaga, it occupied a low-ceilinged room fitted with small chairs that seemed to us to have been stolen from a kindergarten. We were served local red wine, probably their first wine for our youngsters. Not a propitious gustatory introduction for them, I thought. Local musicians entertained us on *guitarras, canas, zampoñas,* and *charrangos* (guitars, flutes, pan pipes, and ukulele-like instruments with armadillo shell bodies).

Christmas presented a challenge, for evergreen trees did not exist in Bolivia. Susan managed to pick up some spruce-like branches from a house near ours where bushes were being pruned. We fastened them to a wooden frame, decorated them with candy, and prided ourselves on our *tannenbaum*. With Maria's help, Susan put together a Christmas dinner that we shared with Gonzalo. After dinner we challenged ourselves as we tried to remember the stanzas of *The Night Before Christmas*.

Once again in Gonzalo's van, we took a weekend in the Yungas. Susan, Alice, and Eric were eager to see the area in which Gonzalo and I worked. "But let's go to the South Yungas," Gonzalo suggested. "There's a nice place to stay in Chulumani."

Gonzalo picked us up early on a Saturday morning. Crowded into his van, we traveled up through Miraflores to the Yungas road. Switchback after switchback, we climbed toward the pass at the *cumbre*.

"There are a lot of llamas here," Eric noted.

"Yes, and alpacas," replied Gonzalo. "The alpacas have longer, richer fleece. You can see that as you look at them. Their wool is preferred for knitting by Bolivian women."

"We don't have them in America—North America, I mean," commented Alice.

"And in South America, we don't have bison or deer or bears or any other large mammals," noted Gonzalo. "Not even raccoons. I guess these various species of mammals evolved after the two continents mostly separated."

Gonzalo stopped the van at the summit, and he took pictures of us standing in front of the 4,650-meter sign. "Is this the highest road in the world?" Eric wondered.

"Aren't there higher roads in Tibet?" queried Alice.

"Well, maybe," Gonzalo replied. "I don't know. And the road to Zongo goes higher than this to a cosmic ray study station built by some French scientists."

"But this is the highest I have ever been," asserted Eric.

"Except in an airplane." Alice managed to get in a last word.

"Okay, kids. Back in the van," I interjected.

We drove down, crossing the large cirque that had been the site of the earlier fuel-related mishap when Gonzalo and I had to coast downhill to buy gasoline from a young boy. Then into rainy Unduavi to pay our toll. Leaving Unduavi, we turned south as the road divided. The road made deep switchbacks as it coursed into and back out of side valleys cut by tributary streams. Lush vegetation and flowers festooned the descending road. Above the road the hillside was cut into terraces. "Coca," commented Gonzalo waving toward a terraced hillside. "The main cash crop of the region. Those coca plants last for seventy, seventy-five years if they are well tended. The farmers pick the leaves three times a year."

"How do they get cocaine from them?" Alice asked.

"Well, I think you can see the first step right over there," Gonzalo replied. We passed what had probably once been a large hacienda house, now in disrepair. A man was sweeping up coca leaves that had evidently been spread on a flagstone terrace to dry. "So," Gonzalo continued, "after the leaves are dry they are crushed and soaked in kerosene to extract the cocaine. Then the kerosene is allowed to evaporate, and the raw cocaine is shipped off. Mostly to Colombia, I think. There it is refined before being sent on to Cleveland Heights!"

We stopped by a waterfall to enjoy the picnic lunch Susan had packed. Blue morph butterflies swarmed around us. A recent hatch, I supposed. I took a picture of Alice standing beneath the branches of a tree-height poinsettia.

Chulumani was built around a central plaza with a church at one side and what I assumed were municipal and other offices as well as shops along the other sides. Palm trees shaded the plaza, and townspeople sat on benches, relaxed on a Saturday afternoon. A few *vendadores* (sales persons) offered their wares at places on the streets bordering the plaza. Susan found an *aguayo* she liked. A youngster of maybe eight years translated Susan's Spanish into Quechua as she bargained and purchased the weaving. "Children learn Spanish in school," Gonzalo commented. "Many adults in rural areas have not learned it."

We drove past the plaza and out of town a short distance to find the lodging Gonzalo had promised us. The Motel San Antonio proved to be a welcome respite from La Paz. Susan and I marveled at the clean rooms and modern fixtures. A shower with truly hot water! Alice and Eric enjoyed its clean swimming pool. They spent hours in it, soaking themselves in a way that reflected the absence of any such opportunities since leaving Cleveland Heights. They swam. They dunked one another. They played a sort of two-person volley ball.

Alice found a group of girls her age and was soon seated on the edge of the pool, legs dangling in the water, busily chatting in Spanish. Eric, we noted, was seated at a small table on the far side of the pool. He and a Bolivian boy were playing chess with a portable chess set presumably provided by the other boy. Eric's Spanish fluency was limited, but the rules of chess were sufficiently international to surmount that handicap.

Sitting at poolside, Susan and I enjoyed cold beer while we watched our frolicking youngsters. We were all amused by the large horned beetles found in the vicinity of the pool; Gonzalo explained that they were called "*rompe focos*" for their habit of flying into lights and breaking the bulbs. In the San Antonio's dining room, we enjoyed dinner, including a bottle of Chilean wine. I could not help but compare that dinner with the uninspiring food served at the Hotel Prefectoral in Coroico.

Soon—too soon, we all felt—it was time to prepare for our return to Cleveland. We brought out from closets the cartons in which our goods had been shipped to La Paz. They were in reasonable shape, and so we set about packing newly acquired possessions into them. The household items they had contained were gratefully accepted by Maria. They would be treasured.

I had arranged for shipment of the cartons, and soon a truck arrived and took them away. Alice and Eric had both made friends at the American Cooperative School, and they promised to write. Similarly, we had met and enjoyed friendship with our neighbors in Obrajes. Taking leave of Gonzalo was heart-wrenching for all of us.

The day came. Gonzalo's van once again transported us, taking us up to the El Alto airport. Shortly we were airborne and headed home.

PART IV

THE ESCAPE, 2007

16

I OPENED MY HOTEL ROOM DOOR in response to the gentle knock. Rosa Maria, the Hotel Europa bar waitress who had served me a pisco sour and peanuts, turned her head, looking up and down the corridor. "Nobody there," she said. "Good. I wasn't followed." She stepped into the room. "I don't think I'm known here, but I'm always careful."

She was wearing a fine brown and natural white alpaca poncho over her waitress uniform, and her high-heeled shoes had been replaced with loafers. I guessed she was probably in her mid-thirties. Pretty. Her dark hair was cut to about shoulder length. Blue eyes. Slender. A nice figure hidden under that poncho. This young woman was not a native Bolivian, I was sure. And I sheepishly thought to myself that a middle-aged, married man should not be looking at the figure of a young woman. But my father-in-law once remarked that his wife should be worried when he stopped looking at pretty young women!

"Hi," she said, with a charming, seductive smile. "I'm Rosemary Murphy. I'm your CIA contact person here in La Paz. Welcome to Bolivia, and many thanks for your help in getting Gonzalo Mamani safely out of the country."

"Well, hi, I guess," I said. "Rosa Maria, Rosemary, Rosemary Murphy, of course. I mean, well, you're not what I expected. Come in and sit down, won't you?" I took my jacket off the arm chair where I had left it, and motioned for her to sit.

"I will sit. Working as a waitress in high heels has its down-sides."

"Can I get you something from the minibar? It seems to be reasonably well stocked."

"Thanks. Is there some wine? Chilean, maybe, not Bolivian—if a place as classy as the Europa even stocks Bolivian wine."

"Seems to be some Chilean. How about Chardonnay? Or there's also some red, I believe." I pulled out several small bottles.

"The Chardonnay would be great."

I took a beer for myself, and found some glasses on a tray above the minibar. I sat on the edge of the bed. "Now, for heaven's sake, clue me in. What is going to happen? And who are you—I mean—"

She smiled and said, "How does a young woman turn out to be a CIA agent? Is that what you mean?"

"Well, yes, I guess. Yeah, exactly."

"Okay. My story first. Then we have some business to attend to. My mother is Bolivian, my father American. I take more after him than after my mom. Dad works in and around Washington. He's a lobbyist representing the interests of several South American companies. Mom does some free-lance translating. I grew up mostly in the States, but spent many school vacations here in La Paz with Mom's family. They live in Calacoto. Mom always talked to me in Spanish, so I am pretty much bilingual, and I speak like a Bolivian—not like a Mexican or Puerto Rican. I went to college at Smith."

"Hey, I went to Yale," I interrupted. "Dated a girl from Smith for a while."

"Yeah. There were a lot of Yalies around most weekends. Well, I decided I wanted to be a nurse, so I transferred to Simmons College in Boston."

"Just down Avenue Louis Pasteur from Harvard Medical School, where I went."

"Right. Anyway, and making a long story short, I was recruited by the CIA and wound up here, where my day job is as embassy nurse. The State Department considers La Paz a hardship post because of the altitude. Not justified in my mind, but I am not about to rock that boat. So, because of the altitude, all the American personnel here get extra pay, and there's a medical clinic here. That's me, and that's my CIA cover. There are a bunch of CIA people at the embassy, all with some sort of made-up-to-sound-important jobs.

"Actually, I have had to do some nurse things at the embassy. You're a TB specialist, aren't you? I think someone told me that."

"Yeah."

"Well, we actually had a case of TB at the embassy last year. Not one of the Bolivian employees—you might have thought it would be—but a state department man assigned here. An American. He presented to me with symptoms so classic that even I, a nurse, not an MD, pretty much knew what he had. Weight loss, cough, and night sweats. That's pretty classic, right?

"You know, I pulled our copy of Harrison's text of medicine off of the shelf in the embassy clinic and looked up TB. Guess who wrote the chapter, I think? Am I right?"

"Depends on which edition. Was it me?"

"Yup. So then I got the INLASA lab to check his sputum, and they found TB bacilli in it. We evacuated him back to the States."

"Okay. Then why the waitress gig?"

"All part of the cover, part of the spook act. I told the hotel folks I needed more money than the embassy pays. Actually, the CIA pays me well, but the hotel doesn't know that. You know, most of the mid- and lower-level folks at the embassy also don't know that I'm CIA. The embassy clinic is only open in the mornings. And it turns out that the bar job lets me overhear conversations that are sometimes interesting and important. People don't think that a waitress really exists, and they talk about all sorts of confidential stuff within my hearing."

Rosemary had kicked off her shoes and curled her feet under her as she sat in the hotel room's only armchair—a comfortable-looking chair for a hotel room. Relaxed, looking even prettier, I thought. She must have a boyfriend somewhere. "Now then," she said, "fill me in more about you and how you know Gonzalo."

"Well," I said, "I'm a professor of medicine in Cleveland, and I run a research lab there. Gonzalo spent a year with me as a fellow in my lab, and we have worked together here in Bolivia, both on the Altiplano and in the Yungas. I spent a sabbatical year here in 1981 and '82. Gonzalo and I did some pretty interesting stuff then—if you're interested in the immunology of tuberculosis, that is."

"And Gonzalo trusts you. That's pretty much good enough for me. In fact, Gonzalo has made it clear he won't leave without you."

"Is it going to be that tricky? Can't he—can't we—just get on a plane and fly out on some pretext or other?"

"No way! Gonzalo is known to the Bolivian security forces. He's being watched and followed. They're tracking him every day, everywhere. If he shows up at the airport, he will be arrested and wind up in the *carcel* (jail). In fact, if we don't get him out of Bolivia soon, like in a few days, there really is not much hope for him."

"Okay, I guess that's why I'm here. So what do I do?"

"You have your passport?"

"Yes, in the safe in the closet there."

"Get it for me."

I opened the safe and gave her my passport.

"Did they tell you to bring extra passport photos?'

"Yeah." I retrieved them from my suitcase and gave them to her.

"Dave should have set you up with a credit card chargeable to the CIA."

"Yes, I have it."

"Let me see it." Rosemary took it, found a piece of note paper from a pad by the phone, and wrote down the card's number and expiration date.

"Now, then, you know where the U.S. Embassy is?"

"On the Plaza Murillo."

"Right. Tomorrow morning meet me there in the plaza at eleven-thirty. There will be people about; there always are on weekends in any open space *Paceños* can find. Sit on a bench. Try to be near a lamppost that has been made a national monument. Rebel Bolivians hung an oppressing ruler there."

"I know it," I commented.

"I'll find you. I will have a new passport with a new name for you, and give this one back to you as well. Also a new credit card with a name to match the new passport. And I'll return this one. The new one will also bill directly to the CIA in Washington with a copy to me here in La Paz. You'll want your real passport and credit card when you re-enter the States. Don't lose them. I don't think I'll be able to fix your Ohio driver's license, so don't get caught by a traffic cop, but I will give you an international driver's license with your new name.

"Your name is going to be Phillip Masterson. It will be on the new passport and credit card I give you. Gonzalo is also going to have a new passport—an American one—and a new name, George Morrison. Both passports will be well used and a little worn and have Bolivian entry stamps and immigration forms included. You are to be two American men touring South America. Good friends on a junket your wives scorned. You're headed to Machu Picchu, at least for starters. But you are to have no contact with Gonzalo until you meet and start your escape, your run to freedom, on Sunday.

"How much money do you have?" she continued.

"Well," I replied, "Dave Swenson, my college friend who turned out to be a CIA person, gave me a thousand cash in U.S. currency, almost all of which I still have. And two thousand Bolivian *bolivianos* and an equal amount of Peruvian *soles*. Plus the credit card."

"Okay. I'll give you another couple of thousand *soles* when I see you tomorrow. You'll be well-heeled. And use the credit card almost every day if you can. Tonight for dinner. Dave checks that account every day. So will I. A simple, easy, but effective way to track you and your progress."

"Yeah, I guess I can do that."

"Go out to dinner tonight. Soon after we finish here. Bolivians don't eat dinner until nine thirty or ten, but Americans are expected to eat earlier. They always do. Talk to the concierge downstairs and get a couple of recommendations. In fact, I want you to be noticed here, so ask about places to eat, things to do on the weekend, whatever else comes to your mind. You are an American businessman, and you want to eat in a nice place and want to enjoy the weekend. You have appointments on Monday and Tuesday; be sure the concierge knows that."

"But I guess I won't be here on Monday and Tuesday."

"Right, but we don't want the hotel to know that.

"When you come back from dinner," she continued, "fish around in your pocket and be unable to find your room key-card. Go to the reception desk and tell them you must have left your card in your room or lost it somewhere. Maybe at the restaurant. They'll give you a second one. I want you to give me that second one when we meet tomorrow."

"So, are we going to have secret trysts in my room?" I asked with what I hoped was humor.

"No, no, none of that. But after you leave, which you will do without checking out, I will come by every evening and rumple your bed to make it looked slept in, run the shower, dampen and discard the towels, things to make the room look used. The hotel folks should not know you have left." More secret spy stuff, I thought.

"Okay," I said. "I meet you tomorrow morning and you give me a new passport and more money. How do I connect with Gonzalo and how do we get out of here?"

"Well, this is the plan. But things may happen, and you will be on your own and should be ready to improvise.

"Tomorrow ask the concierge to have a picnic lunch for you for Sunday. For two. Let him know that you are meeting a *chica*, an *amiga*—a girlfriend—for a picnic up on the road to Zongo. Ask for a bottle of wine, Chilean, not Bolivian, to be included with the lunch. Ask for some flowers—*cantutas*, if they can get them. They're the Bolivian national flower, you know."

"Yes, I remember."

"Then, about eleven o'clock Sunday morning, take the lunch and head out and catch a bus down to Calacoto and all the way to the end of the line. Then walk up to the Valley of the Moon. It's not very far."

"I know it. We used to picnic there sometimes when we lived here in 'eighty-one."

"Take your small day pack. You have one?"

"Yes."

"Pack changes of underwear and toiletries. Wear casual clothes and a warm sweater. You'll not be coming back, and you will be up on the Altiplano where it gets cool." I was glad I had brought along my multi-pocketed outdoor pants.

"As you travel, shower, if you can, and shave every day. Keep up the American tourist act. Look like American businessmen on vacation, not like *muchilleros*," she said, using the local Spanish word for backpackers.

"What about my things? My good suit?"

"Leave them. When you get home, charge replacements to the credit card Dave gave you."

"So then, the hotel won't know I've left."

"Correct, and as I said, I'll come by on Sunday—Monday too, if I can swing it, to mess up your room and make it look lived in," Rosemary added. "Maybe on Tuesday I'll pack up your clothes, take them out and drop your key-card at reception. They have your credit card imprint, so they'll charge your account and not care that you really didn't check out with them."

"And I suppose I will meet Gonzalo at the Valley of the Moon."

"Right."

"But he is going to the States, we hope, and will wind up practicing medicine there," I said. If all goes well, I thought to myself. "He'll need to bring his medical school credentials and stuff. They won't fit in a backpack."

"I'm meeting him after I leave you this evening," Rosemary continued. "I'll get from him all of his important papers plus anything else he really values. It will go out to Dave Swenson in D.C. in the diplomatic pouch on Monday morning. Also, we will Xerox his diplomas and put the copies in the frames in his office so it won't be immediately obvious that he has cleared out taking the originals. And tomorrow we'll get his hair cut in an American style. Then passport photos and a new passport—an American one. Also a green card. When he enters the U.S., however, he should use his real Bolivian passport and name. The green card will let him stay and work until he applies for citizenship.

"I'm afraid Gonzalo will never be able to return to Bolivia," Rosemary said, "unless there is a major change in government, which is not likely. I will also give Gonzalo some money—*bolivianos* and *soles* and some dollars. But you will have most of the cash. You two will be traveling light. I suspect, in fact I'm pretty sure, that there will be times when you will be glad that everything you have with you will fit in your small pack. Oh, and take a roll of toilet paper from the hotel."

"Yes, of course. I've traveled in the *campo* before. Gonzalo has a small pack, I hope."

"Yes, he does. I checked."

"Does Gonzalo have family here? Won't they worry about him?"

"His mother and a sister. I'll fill them in after we know that he is safe in the U.S. His sister is married to General Suarez, whom you worked with. And Gonzalo has a girlfriend—fiancée, actually. They live together. They were planning to be married next month—have already planned a reception and sent out invitations. That's good, in fact, because it implies he will be here. I'll be sure she gets out and joins him in the States after we are sure he has made it. You know, I think I should call his sister and ask her what she knows about wedding reception details. I don't know her well, but well enough to do that. She'll probably report the call to her husband, which will further the idea that he does not think he is in danger here."

"Okay," I said. "You seem to have thought of almost everything."

"That's my job. And I really, really want Gonzalo—and you—to make it out safely."

"All right," I said. "I arrive at the Valley of the Moon with my small backpack and lunch. And there I will find Gonzalo waiting for me?" I queried.

"Or he will arrive shortly."

"Then we eat lunch."

"Yes. And be aware that Gonzalo is now being followed every-where he goes. I told you that. That's one of the reasons we need to get him out now. We believe the Bolivian security guys plan to arrest him soon, Monday, probably. Morales wants a big show trial. You know: 'Bolivian traitor spying for the Americans.' Big headlines. There will probably be a couple of security men dressed casually who will show up at your picnic and take up positions to enjoy the scenery and watch you."

"Oh, good," I commented.

"Relax. Enjoy your lunch and reunion with Gonzalo. Then walk up and along through the Valley of the Moon to where the road comes out on the Palca road about opposite the Mina San Francisco turn-off."

"Okay. I know that road. In fact, Gonzalo took us up to the Inca trail there while we were living here."

"The security 'minders' will follow you, of course. At a dis-creet distance, I hope. Just a bit up the Mina San Francisco road there is a now-unused maintenance building on the right. Not much more than a shed, actually. You will find a blue VW bug parked there. In fact, it's already there. The key is under the driv-er's side floor mat. Get in and drive back into town. Move out. Don't waste time. In Obrajes. Turn into Calle Cuatro."

"I know that street," I interjected. "We lived there."

"Yes, I know," Rosemary continued. "There will be a green, beat-up-a-little-but-still-serviceable Datsun parked in front of your old house. Switch to it and head on up through El Alto and out of town to the lake. The Datsun will be yours to use as you need during your escape from Bolivia. In the glove box you will find papers identifying it as a Hertz rental car. If you take it into Peru, you'll need to present them at immigration. In the end, just abandon it. When you do, take off and throw away the plates, remove all the papers from the glove box, and leave the key in the ignition. The VIN numbers have been filed off, so the car will be essentially untraceable. Whoever finds it will be glad to claim it, take possession of it, I think. As to the VW, leave it on the street in front of your old house, but toss its key someplace where it won't be easy to find. I have a duplicate key, and someone will meet you there or perhaps retrieve it later—after dark—and then we'll hide it until after all of this is forgotten."

"Okay, I guess," I commented.

"From there on, you are on your own. Your destination is Salaverry in Peru, on the coast, a major port, just south of Trujillo. You have ten days to get there. Check into a hotel there called Vista del Mar. Further instructions will get to you there. You must be in front of that hotel at four in the afternoon Tuesday of next week. That's when your next contact will be made. You'll get more instructions then, I believe.

"Salaverry isn't much of a place. It wants to be a resort town, but it doesn't make it. There's a beach, but it's not much. Salaverry is a port for cruise ships, and buses run tourists to the Chimu ruins at Chan Chan. Very impressive, pre-Inca site, I am told. If you have time, hire a taxi and go see it."

"So is the plan to smuggle Gonzalo out on a cruise ship?" I asked.

"I don't know. And that plan won't be told to you until you are safely in Salaverry and out of reach of the Bolivian security agency."

"Yeah, okay. And I meant to ask you. Will the Bolivian bad guys follow us into Peru? And could they arrest Gonzalo outside of Bolivia?"

"Not formally or legally. But they will be armed and ready to put a gun in Gonzalo's back. And there will be at least two of them. They would expect him to be alone. In fact, that there will be two of you might confuse them. But you'll have to judge as you go along whether you should be seen together or not. As I said, you'll be on your own. Figure it out as you go along."

"Any advice on getting to Salaverry on this wild dash?" I asked.

"Well, keep a low profile. Act like tourists, I guess. And importantly, travel by train or bus. Stay away from airports."

"Can I ask a favor?" I said.

"Sure."

"Call my wife, Susan, and tell her I'm okay."

"First thing in the morning. Write down the phone number for me." I gave her the number. She put it in her purse.

Rosemary got up, put on her shoes, and moved to the door. Then she turned. "Thanks," she said, and she planted a kiss on my cheek and left.

My God, I thought, what have I gotten myself into? Then I put my suit jacket back on and headed down to ask the concierge about restaurants.

17

I FOUND AN EMPTY BENCH, sat down, and surveyed the plaza. It was sunny; it always is every day for ten months of the year in the high Andean regions. A couple of boys were kicking a ball back and forth. Throwing a ball is North American; in much of the world, including Bolivia, balls are for soccer and must never be touched with the hands. That is a foul, *"manos,"* Eric had learned while we were living in Bolivia two decades earlier. Couples strolled, two pushing baby carriages. Three men in white were selling ice cream. They had coolers hanging in front of them on wide belts that went around their necks. *"¡Helados!"* they called.

Rosemary came striding across the plaza. She was wearing a poncho, different from the one she had worn the previous evening. As she passed my bench, she stumbled, fell almost to the ground, and managed to catch herself with a hand on the pavement. Without looking at me she said quietly, "Follow me." Then she went on across the plaza and started up the street at the far corner. I stood, stretched my arms, and ambled across the plaza, reaching the corner in time to see her turn into a doorway. Following her, I found myself in the Casa de Murillo, a museum in one of the oldest houses in La Paz. I found her in a quiet corner standing in front of a portrait of a long-gone visage, one of several such paintings. A Murillo family member, I supposed.

"One of those ice cream guys is a Bolivian security person," she said. "He works for ANSEB."

"What's ANSEB?" I asked.

"Agencia Nacional de la Seguridad Boliviana. Bolivian National Security Agency," Rosemary explained. "All Bolivian presidents need some loyal strong men, willing to do dirty work, if necessary. For most of Bolivia's history—at least recent history—that's been the army. But Morales isn't an army person. The army has not tried to throw him out, as they have some presidents, but they also have not gone out of the way to help him."

"So Morales needs his own strong men," I commented.

"Exactly. That one watches the embassy every day, checking on comings and goings, I guess. He knows that I work there. We don't want him connecting you to me. So far, you are not known as other than as a visiting businessman. In fact, probably not known to them at all. You are not connected with us at the embassy. Nor with me. We want to keep it that way."

"Suits me."

"Okay," Rosemary continued. "Here are all the documents I promised. Your two passports—old and new, real and phony—credit cards, everything. Go into the next room, find a quiet corner—nobody comes here much—and check it over. Then come back to me here."

I did as I was told to do. All seemed in order, if any part of this adventure had an understandable order to it.

"All seems to be good," I said, returning to Rosemary.

"Take these maps," she said.

I looked at them. One was a road map of Bolivia. We might need that, I thought. The other was a road map of Argentina. "Argentina?" I said to her. "We're not going out through Argentina."

"Yes, you know that and I know that, but I hope it might mislead others. Leave the map in your hotel room, easily findable, but as though it might have been forgotten. I have had it lying around on my desk in the embassy, easily seen. Actually, the drive to Argentina is an interesting one. Beautiful, if you like deserts. But from Tarija to Bermejo, the border town, the road is straight and open across the Chaco Desert. No hiding places. No way to duck pursuers. So it's not really an option for you. Also, I have had out in view a timetable for the rail line through Cochabamba to Brazil."

"Don't you trust the embassy staff?" I asked.

"In this game, survivors trust nobody!"

"Shit! This is beginning to seem like a le Carré novel."

"Yep. He writes pretty good spy stories."

"And now Gonzalo and I are in the middle of a spy story!" I commented.

"Right, my friend."

18

STILL IN THE MUSEUM, I was standing beside Rosemary, seemingly examining a painting next to the one in which she feigned interest. The ANSEB ice cream vendor started to walk into the museum, but the woman at the desk stopped him. She stood and said firmly, "No food or drink in the museum. You can't come in with your ice cream."

"But...." he started to say. Then, thinking better of it, he turned and stepped out into the street. He would wait there, it seemed.

"I think he'll follow me," Rosemary said softly. "I'll go out and turn up, away from the plaza. Wait a few minutes—maybe ten or fifteen, if you can tolerate all these archaic portraits—and then go out and turn down."

"Yeah, okay. I'll survive the Murillo family."

"There's a pizza place on Avenida Arce, down a bit from the university and across the street."

"Yes, I know it. Or at least I know it if it is the same one that was there twenty-five years ago. Pretty good pizza, as I recall. We went there for dinner from time to time when we lived here."

"Yes, same one, I guess. An Italian family owns it. The son of the original owner now runs it, I think. A family business. And yes, pretty good pizza, although there are now lots of other pizza places in La Paz."

"The only one when we lived here."

"So, treat me to pizza for supper. Six o'clock. Okay?"

"My pleasure."

FRANCESCO'S Pizzeria was much as I remembered it. I climbed the stairs to the balcony sitting area, passing by the ground-floor, wood-fired oven and pick-up counter for take-outs. Where do they get their wood, I wondered. There was a family of six enjoying pizza. Their supper, I supposed, as would be Rosemary's and my pizza for us. No one else was present. Surprising for a Saturday night, I thought, but then it was very early for a Bolivian dinner time.

Pointing to a placard on the wall, a young man with an apron around his waist asked what I would like to order. "My guest will be here shortly," I replied. "Then we'll decide. Now, do you have wine? A Chianti, perhaps."

"Yes, of course. Our Chianti comes from Argentina. We get it at the black market near the cathedral."

"Not Chilean?"

"No. We used to get some Chilean wine, but no longer. It has gotten too costly for us. Our customers wouldn't pay the price we would have to charge."

"Okay. Bring what you have and two wine glasses."

Rosemary—Rosa Maria—arrived in time to welcome the bottle of Chianti. As she sat down, I filled her glass.

"I guess we should order. It will take a little time for the pizza to be prepared," I said.

"Right. How about pepperoni and mushrooms?"

"And black olives," I added.

"Sure, good."

The waiter wrote down our order, walked over to the edge of the balcony, formed our order into a paper airplane and sent it down to the man at the oven on the ground floor.

"Hah!" I said. "I remember that act."

"Oh yes, part of the ambience. In today's world he could have a computer terminal and enter the order into it. But the paper airplane works, is never "down," and is an important bit of theatrics."

We picked up our glasses. "To Gonzalo's successful escape," I said.

"Yes, yes," she said.

"So now," I said. "Tell me more about Gonzalo being a spy and how you have been involved in that. It's okay to talk here?" I asked.

"Yes. It's safe here. No one here will be able to follow an English conversation."

"So, fill me in. You told me the CIA recruited you. And I guess you recruited Gonzalo. But there must be more to it."

"Well, yeah. With my mixed heritage, dual nationalities, and divided loyalties I was an easy target for the CIA recruiters. And an obvious person to send to Bolivia once in the CIA. But there's a lot more to it than just my nationality—or nationalities. I'm an idealist, I guess, and sometimes an optimist. I think things can get better in Bolivia. And I think, really think, that the U.S. can do a lot to help Bolivia. And much of the rest of the world, actually.

"Except for the damn Bolivian politics and the stupid army generals who are power-hungry and mostly motivated by feathering their own nests."

Rosemary was clearly feeling relaxed and ready to unload. Perhaps the wine helped. But, I thought, she probably seldom if ever had a chance to let down her guard like this. "Sure," she continued, "I stumbled into this gig. Or was recruited without realizing what I was getting into. But I was ready and even eager for this. I signed on and got trained. Of course, once it was decided I would go to Bolivia, I didn't need a lot of country-related training. Nor language. You know," she interjected, "the CIA and the State Department often send people off to various countries with little or no language fluency. Stupid!

"Then I met Gonzalo. Just a girl-boy thing that happened casually in a park and led to dating. But he is General Suarez's brother-in-law. Suarez is a biggie. If Morales stumbles, the army will move, and Suarez will be Bolivia's president. How could I not take advantage of that connection? All my CIA training kicked in. I passed on information. I played it for all it was worth. I betrayed a good, fun friendship. Two people, Gonzalo and me, two friends betrayed by me.

"You know," she continued, repeating herself, her tongue loosened by the Chianti but also by what must be have been an almost unique opportunity to unburden herself, "people matter. You matter, I matter, Gonzalo matters. Friends matter, and I betrayed the friendship that Gonzalo gave me. All for what my CIA bosses would call the greater good of the country. Greater good? Maybe. Maybe not. And which country? Especially in my case, which country?

"Now Gonzalo is in trouble, bad trouble, and it's all my fault. You have to get him out!"

"I don't know how much you know about another aspect of this," I said. Then I told her about lithium.

"Well," she said, "that makes it more important, I guess. But it doesn't really change Gonzalo's situation. He has to get out without being caught. You must get him out."

The Chianti bottle was empty. I caught the waiter's attention and paid our bill. "Let me try to get you a taxi," I said.

"No," she said, "I have an apartment on Plaza Abaroa, just around the corner. I can walk." Not very steadily after the Chianti, I thought.

"Well, then, I'll walk you home."

We paused at the entrance to her apartment building. "Meet me here in the Plaza Abaroa tomorrow morning. Nine thirty. I want to be sure we are both on the same page—pages, I guess— for everything in this escape." She turned and looked at me. "As of now, you are on your own." She threw her arms around me. Then backed away and turned to enter the building. "Be careful. And take care of Gonzalo." She had tears in her eyes.

19

THE NEXT MORNING I found an empty park bench in the plaza next to Rosemary's apartment building. The plaza was full of families with children playing games I did not really understand. Rosemary soon came walking toward me. She was wearing tight-fitting jeans, loafers, and yet another alpaca poncho. A very attractive young woman, I once again thought to myself. She sat on the bench beside me. "Do you understand everything? Do you have questions?"

"Yes, I think so. And yes, lots of questions."

"Well, I guess questions are appropriate. But I don't have answers, I expect."

"No, of course not."

"Bottom line is that Gonzalo has to be in Salaverry in ten days. How he gets there—how you get him there—is totally up to you. And whatever you now think you might do is probably wrong. You know Peru well enough to keep moving in the right direction."

"Yes," I interjected. "I have traveled much of the route. But a long time ago." I paused, then added, "I'm sure we can make it. Well, pretty sure."

"And I'm sure, and the CIA is sure. Most of all, Gonzalo is sure. Well yes, pretty sure for all of those, including Gonzalo and me. Pretty sure is all we can ask for, I guess.

"You should know," Rosemary added, "that our information is that ANSEB plans to arrest Gonzalo tonight. Things are unrolling quickly. It's time to get Gonzalo out of here.

"Now, then, go!" We stood. "God be with you. Go!" She strode away.

I took the bus down to Valley of the Moon. Gonzalo was

sitting on a rock ledge when I arrived. We greeted each other warmly, exchanged hugs. "Gonzalo, you look great. Especially for a man on the run!"

"Well, I hope I stay that way—looking great—and on the run! But first, how's Susan, and how are Alice and Eric?"

"All well. They would have sent you greetings, but in fact, only Susan knows I am here, and she does, of course—send greetings, that is."

I set down the lunch basket. "Look at the *cantutas*," Gonzalo said. "Bolivia's national flower. I will miss them. In fact, there is much here in Bolivia that I will miss. I probably will never, ever be able to return to my homeland—to here, to Bolivia."

"Yes, I know. I'm sure it is sad for you."

"It is, but…"

"Over there," Gonzalo cocked his head toward two men. "They are the ANSEB men following me. These days a pair of them is never far away." The two men indicated by Gonzalo were sitting on a ledge about seventy-five yards away and obviously watching us. They were dressed casually, wearing sweaters. Both had *lluchus* (knit hats with ear flaps typical of the Andean region) on their heads; one had a fedora on top of the *lluchu*.

"Do you think they are armed?" I asked.

"Probably. In fact, almost certainly. Even though they know I can't run or go anywhere. But guns are very *macho*."

"Ah, but you can run—and are about to."

"So Rosa Maria told me, but you'll have to fill me in on that."

"Well, we'll be winging it much of the time. But let's start by eating lunch. Should we offer to share with them?"

"*¡Nunca!* You must be kidding."

I opened the lunch basket. "Look at this. Fried chicken and potato chips. I remember potato chips as essentially nonexistent when we lived here."

"Progress. The world of fast food has reached Bolivia."

"And, thanks to the Hotel Europa, a bottle of Chilean wine. Sauvignon blanc—just right for chicken."

We opened the wine and ate our lunch, chatting amiably.

Gonzalo asked about my family. "Susan is busy. She has been recognized as an artist, and there's a lot that goes with that. Alice," I said, "is married to a lawyer and has two children, a boy and a girl. Good kids. Bright."

"Nietos," commented Gonzalo. "Grandchildren! That's wonderful. They should be smart. They have inherited some good genes."

"Right. Thanks. Alice has kept up her Spanish and is teaching English as a second language over in the near west side, the Tremont area, in Cleveland. She loves it, and she really has a talent for teaching. And Eric is a computer scientist out in California. I have no real idea of what he does. It's far beyond me, although he does try to explain it. He's also married, but no children yet. His wife is a real sweetheart. She also works with computers. Programming—or something like that. They have a lovely house; with both of them working in the computer world, they are well off."

I brought Gonzalo up to date on my research. He told me about his current studies of high altitude adaptations. Then Gonzalo asked about Jennifer. "Well," I said, "she's still working with me. She's really first rate. I couldn't function—couldn't keep the lab going—without her."

"I loved her—at least I thought I did," Gonzalo said. "And I treated her badly, very badly."

"She told me about it."

"It was really bad. But I guess it's all past, now.

"Anyway, tell me about our escape plans. I have not been told anything much," Gonzalo continued. "If we didn't get away and I were arrested, then I shouldn't know anything. At least that's how Rosa Maria explained it to me."

I thought about that. I understood that Rosemary was trying to shelter me in case Gonzalo had been picked up before our meeting, but at this point we were on our way together. "Well," I said, "now you need to know. There's a car waiting for us at the other end of the valley, where it comes out on the road to Palca. The key is under the driver's floor mat. We drive out, hopefully leaving your security friends behind. We change cars on Calle

Cuatro in Obrajes. In front of where we used to live. Then out of town. We have ten days to reach Salaverry, on the coast south of Trujillo in Peru. We must be there next week on Tuesday afternoon. Four o'clock, Rosa Maria said. How we get there is up to us. We will certainly be followed by your Bolivian security friends. If they catch us before we get out of the country, they'll arrest us. If we make it into Peru and they get to us there, they'll try whatever they can to get us back into Bolivia.

"The ANSEB agents following us are going to be surprised to find that there are two of us. You are known to them; I am not. I've never been on their radar screen. Hopefully, that will confuse them. Already has, perhaps. And it will make it more difficult for them once we are in Peru. As of now you are George Morrison, an American tourist. I'm Phillip Masterson. We're friends on a trip. Our wives didn't want to join us in this 'out-back' part of the world."

"Rosa Maria explained that to me when she gave me the phony passport and stuff."

"Okay. Something important to understand. If we get separated—and that is not in the plan—the destination is the Vista del Mar Hotel in Salaverry. You'll be contacted there at four in the afternoon on Tuesday next week. What happens after that? I have no clue. Somehow you get to the States. I guess I go home in a normal tourist way. Fly home, I suppose.

"In traveling, we use buses and trains. We stay away from airports. We abandon the car at some early point, I guess. Hopefully in someplace where it won't be found for a while and traced. I guess we should take off the plates and ditch them. We play tourist along the way if convenient—even if not, if awkward. That's what we are supposed to be—tourists. Now you know as much as I do."

"Okay, Phil," Gonzalo said, "let's do it."

We stuffed the remnants of our picnic back in the basket provided by the Hotel Europa and set it on a ledge. We'd be back for it, it seemed. We put our small packs on our backs. That would surprise no one. Nobody with any sense would leave an untended pack anywhere in Bolivia. Then we strolled along the path, talking about American politics as we passed our two watchers. Presently the path descended to an unused road. Easier walking, but no longer suitable for vehicles. We paused from time to time to look at the interestingly sculptured stone walls lining the increasingly narrow valley. The ANSEB men followed us at a reasonable distance, keeping us in view but not interfering with our progress. The path-road turned to the left and climbed uphill. We emerged at the Palca road, the ANSEB agents still at the bottom of the hill behind us. The VW was waiting as promised.

"Go!" I shouted to Gonzalo.

We took off running. At the car, Gonzalo found the keys and jumped into the driver's seat. I climbed into the passenger side. Gonzalo turned the ignition key, put the car in gear, and we roared off toward La Paz. Panting, the two security men reached the road to watch us leave. I turned and saw one of them pull out a hand gun. A shot went high over our heads. The other pulled out a cell phone. "They're armed," said Gonzalo, not looking back as he drove. "That's no surprise. And it probably means that any of them who pursue will also be armed, which may be bad news."

"Yes, but they really want you alive for a very public trial. And that will be true as they try to follow us. And who knows what they are going to do with me!"

"Your being here must really confuse them."

"I suppose. Actually, I hope so."

"They're calling for back-up," I reported to Gonzalo, "and they know what this car looks like. But we'll be dumping this car."

We reached Calle Cuatro uneventfully. There we found the Datsun as promised. Taking the VW keys with us, we changed cars. I got into the driver's seat. "Gonzalo," I said, "get in back and lie down on the floor. They'll be looking for a car with two men in it." A young man came around the corner of the house, jumped into the VW, and drove away.

Without speeding and carefully observing every stop sign and traffic signal, I drove through La Paz and up the road to El Alto. We stopped and Gonzalo moved to the front passenger seat; we would have to stop to pay a toll, and we did not want to attract attention by having him hiding.

Driving up to El Alto and our route to Peru, we could see the crest of the hill-climbing road when we encountered a blockade. Bolivian men and boys were piling old tires across the road. "Damn," said Gonzalo, and he got out of the car and approached a man wearing a *lluchu* who seemed to be the local organizer and the man in charge, if anyone was. They chatted, while I stayed behind the wheel in the Datsun. Gonzalo was earnest, the man with whom he was speaking gestured from time to time. Ultimately, the man called to two teenage boys, and they moved three tires from one end of the blockade, creating a space just large enough for us to pass through. Gonzalo handed the man some money, and climbed back into the car.

"Well," I said, "how did you accomplish that?"

"That man's father is a patient of mine. And it helped that I gave him two hundred *bolivianos*. I hope you have plenty of money. Rosa Maria gave me some, but not much. We're certainly going to need more than I have."

"Don't worry. I'm rich! I'll give you more when we stop and are not being watched."

Then out onto the two-lane gravel road euphemistically named the Pan American Highway heading to Lake Titicaca. I fell in with traffic, hoping not to be conspicuous.

"Hooray," I said to Gonzalo. "We made it. We're out of La Paz and on our way."

"It seems to me," Gonzalo said thoughtfully, "that we should hole up somewhere near the lake. Trying to get to Peru tonight would be tough. Fortunately, this is Sunday. It will take them some time to mobilize more agents."

"Rosa Maria planned it that way, I believe."

"But they will come after us and search thoroughly as soon as they can," Gonzalo added. "You know, I think we should go to Huatahata where my friend and patient, Luis Quispe, lives. He'll help us."

That is what we did, arriving late in the afternoon. Señor Quispe greeted us warmly, politely saying that of course he remembered me. He and Gonzalo walked away from the car talking animatedly, gesturing, and clearly hatching plans. They returned to the car. "Follow me," Quispe said as he strode out down the road. I put the car in gear and followed for about two hundred yards and pulled into a barnyard. Quispe talked with his neighbor, who then opened his barn door, drove a tractor out into the yard, and made a place to hide the Datsun.

"We Aymaras protect one another," Quispe said as we walked back to his house. "My *señora* will have a supper for us shortly. You can spend the night here. I can give you blankets, but we have only a two-room house. You can sleep on the straw in my barn. You should be comfortable. And if the *policia* show up, you can hide there."

We walked down to the lakeshore. I tossed the VW keys into the water. Gonzalo was pensive. "It's a beautiful lake," he commented wistfully. Then he added, "Lake Erie doesn't really measure up!"

In fact, it was not much more than thirty minutes later that two ANSEB agents arrived. Señor Quispe welcomed them. No, he had not seen two escapees. Nor had he noticed a Volkswagen on the road, although lots of traffic went by and such a car could easily have passed without his seeing it. "In fact, I probably would not have noticed it," he added. "Would you like to look around?"

"Not necessary," one of them said, and they drove on. I noted that they were looking for the blue VW, not our green Datsun. I hoped that Rosemary or the man who had taken the VW that we had abandoned in Obrajes would get it hidden away soon, so that they would continue to look for it.

We had a dinner of *chicharrón*, *oca*, and *choclo* (pork rind, an Andean tuber, and corn). Señor Quispe brought out some beer, which we enjoyed. We talked for a while, explaining Gonzalo's situation without saying that he was an American spy. Our host did not ask the nature of Gonzalo's transgressions. The sun set over the lake. We wrapped ourselves in the proffered blankets for the night. Safe and hidden, we thought.

Not yet asleep, we heard the ANSEB men again talking with Quispe. They had evidently returned and were questioning him.

"No, no car is here," he said. "Would you like to look around?" They decided they should, and soon they came into the barn. This may be it, I thought to myself. Gonzalo and I buried ourselves as best we could in the straw. The two agents looked in. One of them swung the beam of a flashlight around the dark room. Fortunately he missed us.

20

AT BREAKFAST OF rice and beans, bread, and cheese, we discussed our options. "If they believe we are headed for Peru," said Gonzalo, "and they probably do, then they'll expect us to drive to Puno and catch the train. We'd have had trouble getting the train yesterday, but we could have reached Puno yesterday, spent the night there, and be ready to take the train today. I suppose they will be there at the station waiting for us today and maybe again tomorrow. And they may check out hotels in Puno."

"Puno is in Peru, isn't it?" I asked.

"Yes, we would clear immigration at Desaguadero—and find out how well our new passports work."

Señor Quispe looked puzzled. "New passports?"

"Don't ask. You should not know if they come back," said Gonzalo.

"I would be pretty sure ANSEB will have agents looking for us at immigration," I said.

"Yes, and that will be true wherever and whenever we leave Bolivia."

"So what other option do we have?" I asked. "We can't stay here in Bolivia."

"I suggest we stay on this side of the lake and drive to Copacabana. We can cross the lake by ferry at the Strait of Tiquina. Then," Gonzalo suggested, "we head to Copacabana. We should be able to get there today, probably by noon. We'll have time for you to see the place, maybe go to the Isla del Sol (Island of the Sun). I expect that they'll have alerted someone at the ferry, but they still think we're driving a VW. Our chances there are pretty good, I think. Better than at Desaguadero, anyway. Then tomorrow we can head to Puno, entering Peru at Yunguyo, a sleepy place, an entry point not used much, I think—I hope. I think that would be the least risky place to go through immigration."

"Sounds like a plan," I said. "A good plan, actually. Let's do it."

And so we did. We retrieved the Datsun, said goodbye with profuse thanks to the Quispes, and drove off for Tiquina. I drove, thinking that somehow that might be better if we were stopped and questioned. The road was not heavily traveled. The Altiplano looked sterile to me, as it always had when we lived in La Paz. Tubers—yucca and *oca*, antecedents of potatoes—grew there, but not much else. We saw llamas and alpacas and a few scrawny cattle. I remembered that the hamburger meat we purchased during our year living in Bolivia needed grease in the fry pan. Better done on an outdoor grill, but few drippings then. We passed two women walking barefoot along the road. One was spinning, using a drop spindle.

"Gonzalo," I said, "there are a couple of things we have to think about and be alert to. I think we should assume that our followers will catch up with us in Copacabana. Maybe not, but we should not relax our guard. Obviously we'll have to find places to stay and to eat. But remember, we're supposed to be American tourists, so we should do touristy things."

"Well, the main thing, the thing Bolivians do, is a visit to the cathedral. There's a dark wood carved virgin there—La Virgen Morena del Lago—and some Bolivians make pilgrimages to light a candle for her. And there's a hill with the Stations of the Cross as you climb up. But unless you're more of a church-goer than I am, I would skip it."

"Let's skip it."

"We can stroll around the plaza and look at religious souvenirs for sale in front of the cathedral. And really, about the only other thing tourists might do would be to hire a boat and go out to the Isla del Sol. You know, that's where the original Inca came from before moving to Cuzco."

"Okay. I think that would be interesting to do. But we'll have to see how the time goes."

"And we'll have to see if any of my followers show up," said Gonzalo.

We were nearing Tiquina, and the traffic slowed, soon becoming stop-and-go. "Are they stopping cars? Looking for us?" I asked.

"No, no," Gonzalo said. "It's always like this. The ferry is nothing more than a raft. It can take one truck or maybe two cars at a time. But the strait is no more than a hundred meters or so across. Just wait, be patient. We'll get there."

But it was not to be so easy. Two uniformed agents approached our car. "May we see your papers, please?" They were courteous, but obviously interested in us. We passed over our American passports and Gonzalo retrieved the bogus Hertz rental agreement from the glove box. "Step out of the car, please." We did so, and were patted down. One of them carefully examined the rental agreement. He pulled out a cell phone from a pocket and made a call, walking away so that we could not hear the conversation. The other man stayed with us while we waited. The agent on the phone opened our passports while he talked. Probably passing on the passport numbers, I thought. I wondered if Bolivia had a centralized, computerized registry that would track passports of visitors. And if so, were our phony passports in it? He paused with the phone at his ear, then nodded and came back to us. He gave us back our passports.

"*¿Que pasa?*" I asked in my halting Spanish. "My friend doesn't speak Spanish," I added.

"We are looking for two dangerous criminals. Two men traveling together."

"But we are just American tourists on our way to Copacabana," I said.

"Why are you going to Copacabana?"

"Just to see it. The travel agent in La Paz said it is a beautiful place."

"And this car?"

"We rented it in La Paz. We'll go back and turn it in again tomorrow."

"Have you seen a Volkswagen on the road?"

"I don't think so, but I haven't paid much attention to other cars. In fact, there hasn't been a lot of traffic."

The two men stepped aside and conferred with one another. Gonzalo looked worried. I was also worried, but I tried not to show it. They handed our passports and the vehicle papers back to us. "Have a good visit in Copacabana."

"Whew," I said. "We passed. But I was on edge."

"You were on edge," Gonzalo said. "I was terrified."

We approached the strait, and the ferry—such as it was—came into view. So also, docked there and ready for our inspection, was the Bolivian navy. The largest ship—there appeared to be three, all together—was, I thought, a World War II American navy PT boat. "Yep," Gonzalo responded to my query. "It was disassembled at Antofagasta, brought here by train, and put back together here. It's the flagship of our navy."

"Why in the world does Bolivia need a navy?" I asked.

"Why so that we can have admirals who can wear uniforms and draw salaries."

"And drive around in those boats."

"Well, I wouldn't be too sure of that. It might be asking a lot of them."

Ultimately it was our turn. We crossed the strait on the ferry-raft and headed up to the right on the road as it paralleled the lakeshore. Then on to Copacabana.

21

WE ENTERED COPACABANA, Gonzalo driving, passing through the central plaza and turning away from the lakefront to look for a quiet and inconspicuous place to spend the night. We agreed that here, in Copacabana, Gonzalo would speak only English and that I would do my best in fragmentary, tourist Spanish.

We would adopt the new personas that Rosemary had given us. We were American tourists.

Not far from the plaza we entered what appeared to be a residential area. Gonzalo drove slowly. We spotted a house with a placard in the window. *HABITACIONES* (rooms). I went in to investigate while Gonzalo stayed in the car. A woman I judged to be about fifty or fifty-five greeted me. I explained in my best broken Spanish with English words mixed in that we were two American tourists in Copacabana for the day and one night before returning to La Paz the next day. We needed a room for the night. Yes, she had a room with two beds on the second floor. Her only other room was occupied by a young tourist couple from Argentina. The bathroom was shared and down the hall from the two rooms.

I waved Gonzalo in, and he walked up to the house carrying both of our packs. She asked for our passports, and then entered us into her registry. "Welcome to Copacabana, Mr. Masterson, and you also, Mr. Morrison. I am sure you will enjoy your visit." She handed me the room key and returned our passports.

"Where can we leave our car," I asked. "Will it be safe on the street?"

"It would be better if you would pull into the drive beside the house and put it in back," she replied.

I liked that option, although I hoped we were still thought to be driving a Volkswagen. "Good. We'll do that."

"What time do you want breakfast?" she asked.

"Well," I said, "we like to get going early." I did not know what time the train we planned to catch to Cuzco left from Puno. It couldn't be much of a drive to get there, but we would have immigration to deal with. And also, I thought, if we are going to face the risk of meeting Bolivian security forces, it might well be at an immigration checkpoint.

"Six o'clock?" she queried.

"Yes, good."

"I think the Argentinean couple also wants an early breakfast," she commented. "I'll check with them when they return.

They're taking a boat out to the Isla del Sol at this time. That's something you should do."

"Do we have to book a tour?" I asked.

"No, just go down to the waterfront and talk to one of the boatmen there. Be sure to bargain. They should come down at least twenty-five percent from their asking price. And be sure you visit the cathedral. It is very famous. Many pilgrims come here to pray to the dark virgin.

"You will be eating dinner at a restaurant?" our hostess asked.

"Yes."

"Get the *trucha*. The trout. it should be fresh from the lake. Excellent. I would not order *carne*. Not when you are here on the lake."

We thanked our hostess, put our packs in our room, parked the car behind the house, and walked into town. We found a restaurant on the plaza and enjoyed lunch. During lunch Gonzalo told me that many years ago someone introduced rainbow trout into Lake Titicaca. The trout did well there, and are now fished commercially.

"Let's go first to the cathedral," Gonzalo suggested. "We should pray there. Are you Catholic?"

"No, not at all."

"Well I guess I am, or was," Gonzalo said, "but I'm not much of anything now. However, if we are going to keep up the tourist act, I think we should light candles and do the proper cathedral thing."

We walked across the plaza to the cathedral. It was surrounded by a fence with a gate that was open. Clustered in the plaza near the gate were half a dozen stalls offering medals, cards, and various other religious items. We each purchased a candle. In the cathedral we lit our candles, tipping their wicks into other candles to light them, and then set them beside the many candles already in place. Gonzalo walked down the center aisle, crossed himself, and genuflected before the altar, then took a seat in the front row. He knelt and appeared to pray. I found a side chapel.

Gonzalo returned to join me. He took my arm and steered

me to a quiet corner at the back of the sanctuary. We sat in a pew. We were essentially alone. There was only one worshipper present, an elderly woman in a pew near the front. "Now, then," Gonzalo said, "there are some things I have to tell you." Things I didn't already know, I wondered. "Bolivian politics are always complicated, and Morales's election has made them more so."

"Yes, I know that, I understand that. What I don't understand is how and why you got involved in this espionage business. How did you become an American spy?"

"Well, there's a lot about that that you don't know. And I think now you should. Confession time, I guess, which sort of seems right in this cathedral.

"My sister is married to General Alberto Suarez. Remember him? We worked with him during our studies—he was a colonel then—and I think my sister may have met him during that time. Anyway, they're married and have a couple of kids. Two or three times a month, I have dinner with them. Discussions often turn to Bolivian politics, and I keep my ears open. Even now, even after Morales's election, the army is a major political force. Despite Morales, all Bolivian politics involve the army—always have, still do, and probably always will. Don't forget, the army has forced changes in Bolivian governments many times. It can never be discounted, although you Americans seem to have trouble accepting that—"

"Yes, I know," I interrupted. "I do accept the role of the Bolivian army in national politics, but then I have lived here."

"Suarez tells his wife and the word gets to me that he is a nobody in the army. Just another man who likes to wear a uniform and be paid a general's salary. But I have overheard enough to know that he is a king-maker, that behind the scenes he is a major player. Moreover, he seems to be able to keep everyone happy, both his fellow army generals and Morales's *campesino* lieutenants.

"So, in the course of dinner-time conversations at my sister's house, I have learned things. Much—most—of what I learned I reported to Rosa Maria. But some I didn't. Maybe I thought that what I heard was too indefinite, too vague, for Americans to worry about. Sometimes I thought it might be too damaging. Or even dangerous to her. Moreover, I thought my information might provoke American reactions that would be bad for Bolivia. Maybe it wasn't my place to make such decisions, but I did. I am, after all, a Bolivian, and proud of it.

"Much of what I kept to myself focused on Bolivia's growing alliances with China—secret alliances. Venezuelan money has bankrolled Morales. But Morales is smart enough not to put all his eggs in that basket. I'm worried about that. The U.S. knows about it, but they don't know details. I have heard my brother-in-law make remarks that might provide insights, but sometimes they seemed too speculative for me to pass on. Maybe that was wrong, but that's what I did. Maybe I should have tried to pass on everything."

"Okay," I said, "but how did you get involved with the CIA in the first place?"

"You know," Gonzalo said, "it's clear to me now, but I almost didn't know it was happening at the time. I met Rosa Maria, probably not by accident, looking back on it. She's American and I had spent a year in Cleveland with you. We met in a park in Sopacache, I think. Soon, I started dating her. We had lunch together, once I think. I liked her. So I went to the Europa bar a couple of times, and then one thing led to another.

"Before long she had recruited me. I guess it was easy. Morales had not yet been elected, but I was pretty certain that someone like him would be. And that, I believed—still believe—would not be good for Bolivia. And then, there was the money, lots of it, more than I could imagine, and in American dollars. I'm a rich man!"

"Stashed away some place safe, I hope."

"Oh yes," Gonzalo replied. "In a bank account in Grand Cayman. You know that there is a *cambio,* a money changing office, just around the corner from the U.S. embassy. Next to a bookstore."

"Yes."

"Upstairs, over the *cambio* and bookstore is the office of Señor

Francisco. He has a last name, I guess, but he doesn't give it to his clients. He is a money changer. He owns all of the *cambios* in La Paz and changes foreign currency for the hotels. For a commission he will set up a numbered, anonymous bank account in Grand Cayman, or elsewhere if you prefer."

"Your 'rainy day' fund," I said.

"Right, and I'm in good company. I am certain that General Suarez has such an account somewhere. So also, I would guess, does Evo Morales. All Bolivian politicians have retirement plans outside of Bolivia, often in Argentina, sometimes in Spain. And they all have funds secreted that will let them enjoy retirement.

"Well, the point that matters now is that the Bolivian security people know I was, still am, I guess, a spy. But they don't know what I know and what I don't know, much less what I might have passed on. That's why they want me alive. They want to take me back to La Paz, put me in prison, and then torture me until I tell them all I know. And where I have been getting my information. If they find out, it will not only be bad for me, but also bad for my sister and her husband, General Suarez."

"Okay," I said. "Okay, confession time. I'm glad you told me that. Now I will tell you what more I know that you may not know. The CIA is the American intelligence agency. Rosa Maria is the CIA agent in Bolivia."

"Yes, I know that. I told you. I am a spy, and she is my contact person."

"Right, and the CIA wants to rescue you, to get you out of Bolivia, to get you safely to America. That's why I am here. That's what we're trying to do now. That's why we have to get to Salaverry. You'll be picked up there somehow."

"Yes, I know that. At least I hope that is so."

"And you ought to be wondering why the CIA wants to rescue you. Well, there are a couple of reasons. For one thing, I am sure that they'll want to talk with you, to 'pick your brain,' as the current slang expression goes. Find out what you know about Bolivia's government under Morales. From what you have said, I would guess they want to know as much as you can tell them about General Suarez. He seems to me to be a key player. Suppose the military decides it is time for Morales to go. Would Suarez then become president?"

"Yes, I think he might. And what you suggest is not really far fetched. The Bolivian army is the country's main political party, if you want to think about it that way. And Suarez is a top dog in the army."

"Okay," I continued. "There is also the fact that the CIA is an American agency staffed by Americans. It simply does not sacrifice its agents. Not an American thing to do. And also, who knows what you might reveal if captured. You might compromise Rosa Maria and the entire CIA intelligence operation here in Bolivia. The other reason, a major reason—important to them, I understand—is lithium."

"Lithium!" Gonzalo's face expressed surprise.

"Yes, lithium. It is a key element in all light-weight, long-lasting batteries. Important to America's space program. Important to our defense systems."

"So?"

"So, the major sources of lithium in the world are Bolivia, North Korea, and China," I said. "The U.S. has some, but not in lodes worth mining."

"China," Gonzalo said. "Okay. I get it. I can see that Morales' developing liaisons with China are important to America. I wish Rosa Maria had told me this. I might have found out more."

"She probably didn't know," I said. I rose to leave, ending our conversation, our confessions.

"So, now," Gonzalo said, "while we're being religious, let's go do the Stations of the Cross."

"Really? I thought we would skip them."

"Yes. I understand—well, I think I was told in one of those high school wonderful Bolivia classes—that the Stations of the Cross here are world famous. So you must have heard of them, No?"

"Maybe I was home sick from school that day!"

"Well, they're here, not far from the cathedral. They are

located along a trail that climbs some hill, and the view from the top is supposed to be great."

"Okay," I said, "for the view. But I think we might skip the religious icons or whatever of that sort there is. So I guess we should ask someone and see where they are."

A woman selling religious trinkets pointed to a hill. "Over there. Up the Cerro Calvario, Calvary Hill." We found the trail and dutifully noted the twelve sculptured representations of Christ's journey to crucifixion. At the top we looked out at the lake. A magnificent, panoramic vista. Both the Isla del Sol and the Isla de la Luna were easily seen. "Isla del Sol next," I said.

We walked back to our rooms, intending to use the lavatory there before taking a boat to the Isla del Sol. I was in the upstairs hall when two men entered the rooming house and talked to our hostess.

"*Buenas tardes, Señora,* we are from ANSEB, the Bolivian National Security Agency." They presented credentials to her. "We are looking for two men who are dangerous escaped criminals. We think they may be here in Copacabana."

She replied, "My only guests today are a young couple from Argentina and two American men who are tourists."

"These American men, what kind of car are they driving?"

"Just an ordinary car. Green, I think. It's parked out back. You can look at it, if you want."

"Not a Volkswagen?"

"You mean one of those humpy things people call *bichus?*"

"Exactly. Bugs."

"No, it's not one of those."

"Are you sure these men are not Bolivian?"

"Well, only one of them speaks Spanish," she said, "and it is pretty rough. And they have American passports. Here, this is my registry with their passport information."

They looked at the registry and wrote down our passport numbers. They thanked our hostess and left.

Gonzalo returned from the lavatory. "They're here." I

recounted what I had overheard to Gonzalo. "The good news, I guess, is that they seem to think we're still driving the VW."

"Well," he said, "we have to hope they are not the same men who saw us in La Paz. Then they might know what we look like. And I guess we should just go on behaving like tourists."

"Let's go find a boat to take us to the Isla del Sol."

The beach was shingle, rather than sand. Boatmen had their craft drawn up on the shore. Small boats with outboard motors. We wandered among them, choosing one that seemed—or at least we hoped—might be water-tight. After some bargaining, we agreed on a price. Our skipper called to a teen-aged boy, who would evidently serve as crew, and we were soon under way. The role of the boy signed on as crew soon became apparent. His duty was bailing, which he did assiduously and constantly with a battered coffee can.

"So," I said to Gonzalo, "tell me about the Incas. And why are we going to the Island of the Sun? Why is it important? What's interesting there?"

"Okay, but understand that what I know is pretty much what I remember from grade school history classes. And that's not much."

"Yeah, but it's more than I know."

"Well, the first Inca was born on this island. Maybe. If I remember what I was told in third grade. Inca, that is, the Inca, the ruler of the people we now call Incas. But back then, Inca meant the person, the chief. His father was Inti, the Sun God; his mother was Pacha Mama, the earth goddess. His name was Manco Capac, I think. Anyway, he collected his followers and led them to Cuzco. With subsequent rulers—all called Incas—they conquered everyone in the Andes and established an empire reaching from modern Colombia to Chile. They lasted until the Spaniards— Pizarro—conquered them. These people we call Incas today were remarkable. They built roads everywhere."

"Yes," I interjected, "you took us to one when we lived here."

"And they had a system of mathematics and language of a

sort that used knots tied in cords. You know, I should know more about Incan history, but I'm afraid I don't."

We were about halfway to the island when I noticed that we were being followed by the two men who had presented themselves at the rooming house as agents of ANSEB. They were not close, but would surely catch up with us on the island.

"We have an escort," I said to Gonzalo as I pointed to the boat following us.

"Hmm."

We pulled up to the small dock at the island. Rising up from the shore was a broad stairway. "Go up to the top, and wait for me there," said Gonzalo "Take a good look at the stone work of the stair. It's Incan. But now, give me two hundred *bolivianos*."

As directed, I climbed the stair and waited at the top. The stone work was truly impressive. Worth the boat trip, I thought, although it would have been better had we not been accompanied by our followers. At the dock, Gonzalo was talking animatedly with our boatman. Gonzalo gave him the *bolivianos* I had provided and then raced up the stairs. "Follow me," he said, catching his breath. We ran along a path that went off to the right and then down to another dock, a smaller dock, clearly not the principal one. Our boat was there. We tumbled in and headed back to shore. Looking back, we saw the other boat at the dock, waiting for its passengers.

"So what's going on? What have you done that cost two hundred *bolivianos*?" I asked Gonzalo.

"Well," Gonzalo said with a smile, "I gave up being a tourist. I explained to our boatman that the wife of one of the two men behind us prefers to sleep with me rather than her husband. He is angry and is now chasing us. And I thought he might have a pistol. He works as a file clerk at the ANSEB headquarters and has managed to make some phony but authentic-looking credentials, which he might present. I have no idea whether our skipper believes any of that, but for one hundred *bolivianos* he is ready to accept it as the Gospel truth."

"And the other one hundred *bolivianos*?"

"Ah, yes. Well it seems the other boat with the ANSEB men is going to have a major problem with its outboard motor on the way back. They will have to row back to shore!"

22

WE FOUND A RESTAURANT fronting on the plaza and took a table near a window where we could watch the plaza. As suggested, we ordered trout. It came and looked delicious. Then I noticed the ANSEB agents in the plaza. "Look," I said to Gonzalo, "there are now four of them." They walked slowly around the plaza, and it was apparent that they were looking into restaurants. "Uh-oh! Bad news. Dinner will have to wait."

"Or we'll go hungry," Gonzalo commented.

I put some *bolivianos* at our place, and we walked back past a restroom into the kitchen. "Stop, you can't come in here!" But we did and hastily made our way out a back door.

"Now what do we do?" I said.

"Come," Gonzalo said. I followed him.

"Do you know where you're going?" I asked.

"No, but neither do they!"

We wandered in and out of Copacabana's streets, eventually finding our way back to the beach. It was getting dark, and we sat on a bench, hoping night would make it easier to get back to the rooming house unobserved. Presently two of the ANSEB men appeared. We scuttled off the bench and lay down in a pile of trash at the base of some bushes. They searched the area, waving their flashlights. In fact, the beam of one of them crossed us, but we were not noticed, and the men walked away. Maybe they're getting tired and less attentive, I hoped to myself.

We were about to get up from our hiding place, when the two men returned. Once again we lay still in the trash under the bushes. Once again the flashlight beam swept across us. Once again we escaped notice. I have had enough of this, I thought to myself. But there was more to come. One of the ANSEB men returned yet again. Turning his flashlight on our hiding place under the bushes, he spotted us. "I thought I saw you there. Out! Now!"

"Don't move," I whispered to Gonzalo, and I rolled out onto the beach. I got up, stumbling as I did so, then catching myself.

"I'm hiding from my wife," I said to the agent, slurring my words.

"Your wife!"

"*Sí*. I was in town. At a bar. I had some *chicha* (an Andean drink brewed from corn). Then some more *chicha*," I added with a grin, staggering down to the water's edge so as to lead him away from still hidden Gonzalo. "Then some pisco. Maybe more pisco, I think, maybe. Now I'm too drunk to go home and face my wife. And she is certainly out looking for me. So I came here to hide. And it seemed like a good idea to lie down and rest. Maybe sober up. Maybe sleep."

The agent seemed confused. He appeared not to have noticed Gonzalo still hidden under the bush. He scratched his head. I was pretty sure he had no real reason to suspect me. He didn't know who I was nor what I looked like, and I clearly was not Gonzalo. But I was also pretty sure that he didn't believe my story.

Suddenly Gonzalo burst forth from under the bushes and charged into the agent with a force that could have earned him respect on a North American football field. The hapless agent collapsed and fell into the water. Gonzalo and I took off running until we reached the plaza, where we settled down to a leisurely stroll. It was becoming dark. Two local men out for an evening walk, perhaps.

"I hope he didn't get too good a look at you," Gonzalo said.

"Well, we can't do much about that now," I replied. "You were magnificent."

"I saw that sort of stuff in American football while I was in Cleveland. Never thought I'd be doing it myself. Our sport, our *futbol*, is not that rough."

"Well," I said, "things have changed a bit. They now know that there are two of us, that they are not just searching for you. That is, if those guys talk to one another."

Watching our surroundings, we made our way back to the rooming house.

"Did you have a good day?" our hostess greeted us.

"*Si, claro*," I replied.

"And did you get out to the Isla del Sol?"

"Yes. Very impressive. The Inca steps there are amazing. And we went to the cathedral."

"Good. Good. I'll have breakfast for you at six in the morning."

We retired to our room. I slept soundly, and I was sure Gonzalo did as well.

23

WE HAD PUT COPACABANA but a short distance behind us on the road to Peru, when we found all traffic stopped. I got out of the car and walked ahead. The ANSEB men were there, all four of them. I returned to Gonzalo. "They're examining everybody and searching all the cars," I reported. "Do we brave it? Can we bluff our way through?" I asked with doubt in my voice.

"We'll never get through this way. We have to turn back. We don't have a choice."

I pulled the Datsun out of the line, backed and turned once, and headed back to Copacabana. "I think all of them are there, checking cars," I said. "That means we should have a clear shot at getting out of town the other way. I guess we're going back the way we came."

"Okay," rejoined Gonzalo. "But not to Peru today, I think. Let's go back to Huatahata and my friend Luis Quispe. We can spend another night there and go out around the lake tomorrow."

"Yeah. I'm not sure we have any other alternative. Then I guess around the south end of the lake tomorrow to Desaguadero. I would have thought that would be the riskier way to approach Peru. But if all the ANSEB focus is here on Copacabana, it may be okay. It will have to be! We don't have much of a choice. We'll lose a day that way, but we should still make Salaverry on time."

"Lunch time," I said, as I pulled the Datsun to a stop in front of a low adobe brick building displaying a Pepsi-Cola sign.

"Do you think it's safe to leave the car out in view?" Gonzalo asked.

"I hope so. There's not much else we can do with it. Hopefully, they're still looking for a VW."

We walked in and greeted a woman behind a counter. There were four tables surrounded by chairs. "What do you have for *almuerzo?*" I asked.

"Today, lunch is chicken soup." Then she chuckled. "Of course, I have chicken soup every day. My menu never changes."

"Perfect. A bowl for each of us, please. And some bread. And beer."

The soup was delicious, with large pieces of chicken in it. And the bread was still warm from the oven.

After our meal we drove on to Huatahata, once again to impose on Señor Quispe and his wife. We found Quispe mending fishing nets. "Well, my friends, welcome back. Not yet in Peru?"

We explained about the blockade on the road out of Copacabana. "So we find ourselves once again imposing on your kindness."

"Not at all. Not a problem."

Once again we secured the Datsun with a neighbor. Once again our host offered us beer, which we gladly accepted. As we sat on a bench, Gonzalo began to recount his tale—our tale—to Quispe. "You know," he said, "that I am a wanted man. They are saying that I am a dangerous criminal. That's to scare you. I am not dangerous. I am not a criminal, at least in the usual sense. What I am, what I have been, is an American spy passing what information I can gather to the American CIA. I am paid for doing that, but the money is not important. I spent a year in Los Estados. America is more prosperous than Bolivia, a better place for ordinary people to live. Bolivia has natural resources, lots of them. But Bolivia has corrupt politics, and that is why we get nowhere. America has honest politicians."

"Mostly," I interjected.

"America is a democracy, maybe not perfect, but pretty good.

I want America to have as much influence in Bolivia and on our politicians as it can. That is why I am an American spy. Not for America, but for Bolivia."

"Well," said Quispe, "I am with you. In fact, I'm like an American. I have a business. Not just my farm here, but my launch. I take tourists out to the islands, out to see reed boats being built. And," he continued, "my daughter is in America. She's a student at UCLA in California. She studies economics, whatever that means. She has a *novio* there. I hope she marries him, but even if she does and invites me, I will stay in Bolivia. I belong here. But it is good for young people to get out—if they are smart enough to do something other than pick strawberries in California."

"Maybe some of them should come back to help Bolivia," Gonzalo said.

"Yes. That's true. But not my daughter.

"*Bueno,*" Quispe continued, "it's early afternoon. There are some interesting ruins on small islands that almost no one ever visits. I'll take you to see them. Then dinner and after that back to your hiding place in the hay." Señor Quispe led us down to his launch and soon we arrived at the island of Calauta. "Everyone goes to Suriqui to see the reed boats being made. You've both been there, no?"

We both indicated we had.

"I take many tourists to Suriqui, but nobody wants to go to Calauta. But it is very interesting, very old, long before the Incas." We wandered about the island, awed by the mostly intact ancient ruins. Buildings, houses perhaps, now lacking only roofs that were probably thatch. We encountered a boy herding sheep, using an *honda* to keep them from wandering. Señor Quispe put a stone on top of a rock pillar about four feet high. He pointed to it while motioning to the boy. The boy picked up a stone, put it in his sling, and hit the stone squarely, knocking it off of the pillar. Well, I thought, he could have joined David against Goliath!

Back at the Quispe home, Señora Quispe told us that two ANSEB agents had come by asking questions. "I told them you had taken a group of four German tourists out to see the reed boats being made."

After dinner we returned to the barn where we had hidden previously. "My dog, Galleta (Spanish for cookie or biscuit), whelped last evening. Five pups, one born dead. She is nursing the others on a rug just inside the barn door. Go in slowly and let me introduce you to her." Inside the barn, Quispe petted the dog while Gonzalo and I each let Galleta smell our hands. "You'll be fine now. Get settled in the hay. If the ANSEB men come back, Galleta and I will deal with them."

We had not been long at our resting place in the hay when we heard voices at the doorway. "If they are hiding in this area," we heard Quispe say, "they are unlikely to be in this barn. My bitch whelped last evening. She's just inside the door, and she would not let any stranger in." One of the men—evidently from ANSEB, but not one familiar to us—stepped part way into the door. Galleta growled, loudly and menacingly. The agent took a step backward. Galleta continued her growling. The agent took out a flashlight, scanned the barn quickly, and then backed away.

"Who is it you are looking for?" Quispe asked.

"Two men, one of them a vicious and dangerous criminal. Violent, an evil man. We don't know much about the other man, but he is probably also a criminal."

"Well," Quispe said, "I hope they don't show up here."

"There's a reward for them. Thirty thousand *bolivianos*."

"Wow! That's as much money as I get in a year. What would I have to do? Capture them somehow? But if they're dangerous… Are they armed?"

"No you don't have to capture them yourself. Just tell us where they are so we can handle them. I don't know if they are armed, but I think you should assume they are."

"So if I see them, or think that I see them, I should call you."

"Right. And then try to keep them under observation. And be careful. They are dangerous. Here. The number to call is on this card."

"You know," said Quispe, "there are a couple of unused sheds down by the lakeshore. If I were trying to hide here, I might go there."

"Thanks. We'll check them out."

"And if the criminals are hiding there, I'll get thirty thousand *bolivianos.*"

"You will. Oh, and keep your eyes open for a blue Volkswagen. We believe they are driving one. Although they could have switched cars, somehow."

The two ANSEB agents went to the lake to check out the sheds Quispe had told them of. Finding no one, they departed, once again urging Quispe to report us. After they had left, Quispe came to the barn to report to us. "You two are worth a fortune," he said.

"I'll tell you what," I said. "Give me your daughter's contact information in California. I'll try to get the CIA to send some reward money to her."

"Okay. But I do what I do for friendship and for Bolivia. Not for money."

"After breakfast tomorrow," I told Quispe, "we set off for Desaguadero, this time not through Copacabana but around the southern shore of Lake Titicaca."

"Fine. Should be an easy drive."

24

WITH OUR PROFUSE THANKS and hosts' hopes for success in our ongoing travel, we left Huatahata after an early breakfast. We drove toward Desaguadero and Puno. I was at the wheel. Gonzalo was deep in thought, his left hand against his forehead. "Tiahuanacu," Gonzalo said. "It's not far off the road, and it's part of my ethnic heritage. I'd like to see it one last time."

"I'm not sure," I said. "Maybe we can make the Puno train today. But not if we stop. I think we should just keep going."

Gonzalo said nothing, thinking about the road ahead, I supposed. Maybe even his future after leaving Bolivia. Then he sat upright, straight and rigid, put both hands on the dash board, and exclaimed abruptly, "Stop! Stop the car. Now!"

I pulled to the roadside. Gonzalo opened the passenger door, got out and walked back along the roadside. After about one hundred feet he turned, walked back partway, turned again. He paced back and forth for what was probably no more than five minutes, but seemed much longer.

"Tiahuanacu." Gonzalo said with emphasis as he got back into the car. "We stop and visit it. I'm leaving my homeland forever. You have to understand that. I want to stop. If we miss today's train, there'll be another tomorrow."

"But...."

"No buts. We stop."

"Okay. We'll do it, but I don't really like the idea."

"Screw it! I'm as anxious to get out of Bolivia as you are to get me out. But we're still here. And I'm still Bolivian. What you like or don't like is too bad. We go to Tiahuanacu."

I did not reply to my friend's outburst. Gonzalo was quiet for several minutes. Then he said, "You know, the skills of my ancestors were amazing. That they could have built Tiahuanacu blows my mind. It is built of huge granite-like stones. Those stones were not quarried locally. It is supposed that they were transported on rafts across the lake to this area. But the lake is a fair distance from the ruins."

"Maybe the lake level was different then," I offered.

"Maybe, but that would have to mean an outlet other than Desaguadero. And I don't think one has been found."

"Where does the water leaving the lake at Desguadero go?" I asked.

"To a salt flat where it evaporates and adds to the salt. Not much salt, really. Lake Titicaca is fresh water. But over centuries and millennia—

"So they managed to get the huge stones here," Gonzalo continued. "Then they carved them. Who knows how? Who knows with what tools?"

"I remember. Monoliths, like Easter Island, sort of."

"Yeah. I guess you could say so. The Spaniards defaced them. They carved crosses on all of them and cut up the faces. They thought they were serving God by destroying pagan idols.

"But there is much, much more. Most of it has been excavated since you were here. They built a substantial terrace with the big monolithic idols on it. And other structures, houses perhaps, terraces. There is a sunken terrace with carved heads in its walls. Hard to know much about that, because early and stupid, uninformed attempts at restoration made a mish-mash of it."

"I remember it. Weird."

"Yeah, weird. Now things are being done better—being done right—as they should be. Archeologists from both Harvard and the University of Pennsylvania have worked here with the Bolivian archeology team."

"You know," I commented, "back in 1981, when we were living here in Bolivia, I got together with Professor Julio Ramirez, a pathologist from the university, and we looked at all the vertebrae from the available skeletons. At least those they had then. There was nothing that I thought looked like the typical lesions of spinal TB. But you know, TB has been found in Andean mummies from about that period. In fact, American and Peruvian pathologists have carefully dissected and examined several Andean mummies. They carefully rehydrated lung and bony tissues and then studied them under microscopes. Those pathologists found typical lesions of tuberculosis and even bacilli that stained like TB. More than that, they recovered DNA of tubercle bacilli. Despite those who argue that tuberculosis was brought to the Americas by European colonists, TB might well have been here, probably was, certainly was, in fact long before anyone from Europe came on the scene." I hoped Gonzalo was impressed by my erudition and knowledge of pre-Columbian medical history. I felt very smug!

Shortly, our conversation was interrupted as we turned into the entrance of the Tiahuanacu site. There was a small building, a kiosk but no more than a shed. A man wearing an old suit coat and a *lluchu* was sitting on a bench in front of it. He was whittling with a pocket knife and picking his teeth with a small stick he had sharpened. Tacked up on the wall of the kiosk was a poster with Gonzalo's not-very-good likeness on it. It advertised the thirty thousand *boliviano* reward.

He waved us on into the ruins. Then he stood up, looked at Gonzalo's picture, and turned back toward us. I did not wait for him to look at Gonzalo again.

We parked the car and wandered around. There were no other visitors present. I was surprised—amazed—at how much had changed since my family and I had visited it in 1981. What was then a hill, thought perhaps to hide a pyramid, was now a terraced residential complex. Puma Punka, represented then by only a few carved stones, was now revealed as a large elevated plaza. "Whatever is known or not known about the people who lived here," I commented to Gonzalo, "they certainly were accomplished builders. Look at the size of some of these stones."

"Right," Gonzalo commented. "Somehow they managed to move twenty-five-ton stones across the lake to this place. On reed boats, do you suppose? It doesn't seem possible."

We ambled around the site, and I noted many changes since I had visited with my family more than twenty-five years earlier. Bolivian archeologists had been at work, in company with North American ones, Gonzalo noted. The sun and moon gates with their enormous lintels were as I remembered them. Also the monolithic figures. "Notice the crosses that I told you about, chiseled into the sides of these figures," Gonzalo commented. "The Spaniards did that. They thought they would somehow Christianize them this way.

"These people were not just builders" he continued. "They were architects. In fact, a whole civilization. And all well before the Incas. I guess the Incas ultimately conquered Tiahuanacu. At least I suppose so, but I don't really know. They conquered everything else around the lake—and everywhere else they went. But, you know," he continued, "this civilization may have been pretty much in decline by the time the Incas got here. That's what I was told when I was in school, but I don't remember being given any explanations for it.

"Anyway, the Incas imposed the Quechua language on all those whom they conquered, including remaining residents in this region, I think. But not the Aymara along the shore of the lake over by Huatahata. The Aymara there were skilled healers, and so the Incas left them alone to practice their healing arts. At least that's what my Aymara parents told me when I was a boy. We're proud of being Aymara."

As we were about to leave, we were approached by a boy whom I assumed to be in his early teens. He unwrapped a clay head from a dirty cloth in which it was hidden and asked us if we would like to buy it from him. *"Muy viejo, muy autentico,"* he assured us.

"No, hijo," Gonzalo said, patting him on the shoulder. Turning to me, he commented, "Well, I guess it is authentic in having been made by an indigenous person here—perhaps his father."

As we drove out of the site, we encountered the tooth-picking man at the entrance kiosk. He held a rifle cradled in his arm; an old one, I judged. "That's an old Enfield, I think, except I really don't know one rifle from another," Gonzalo commented. "Back in the sixties, when Barrientos was president, he gave rifles to *campesinos* who supported him. If he tries to shoot it, it is probably more likely to explode than actually fire a bullet. In fact, I would be surprised if he has any bullets for it."

The guard, if he could be called that, stepped into the road, stopping us. I rolled down my driver's window. "You," he said, "pointing at Gonzalo. You are the wanted criminal."

"What are you talking about?" I said. "Let us through. We have to get back to La Paz."

"But he's the man in the poster. A dangerous criminal."

"Look, my friend," I said with annoyance in my voice. "We are Americans. Tourists. Not dangerous criminals. My friend doesn't speak Spanish. Please step aside and let us pass. And what poster are you talking about?"

"There." He pointed to the poster offering a reward for Gonzalo and pulled out his cell phone.

"Well," I replied, "that's certainly not us. I really don't know what you're talking about." I pulled the Datsun onto the berm, driving around him and back onto the road to the highway. The guard pointed his gun at us and fired. To my surprise, the ancient gun actually launched a bullet. The missile hit the road behind us. As we drove on, the guard seemed to be reloading the weapon, but we were back on the highway before he was ready to fire the gun again. And he had a cell phone out. "I suppose he is calling us in to the number on the poster. Hoping for some reward money, maybe."

"I don't like being famous," Gonzalo said, "and now they will know that we are headed for Puno. And no longer in a VW."

"Yeah, but I think they should have already figured that out. Where else would we go? And you will just have to take your fame where you can find it!"

"I'd rather not."

25

BACK ON THE SO-CALLED Pan American Highway, we drove on toward Desaguadero and the Peruvian border. Gonzalo was silent, pensive. It must be sad, I thought, to be leaving one's homeland forever. What would I feel if I had to leave America and move to—well, anyplace?

After our visit to Tiahuanacu, it was late in the morning when we approached the border. We were making good time, I thought, but we probably would not reach Puno in time to catch the Cuzco train today. And the good time we were making would not last. We were in sight of the Bolivian emigration point, when we were stopped at a road block. Two uniformed officers approached the car. Not the usual plain-clothes ANSEB agents, I noted. "Please get out and step away from your car," one of them commanded. Passports in hand, we did so. "Open the trunk, please." The two men were courteous, but firm and commanding. They searched the car, examining the back seat and the trunk. One of them used a flashlight to look under the car. "The auto registration, please."

We gave them the Hertz documents. We also gave them our American passports and explained that we were American tourists heading for Cuzco and Machu Picchu. They looked at us carefully, and compared us with a long out-dated picture of Gonzalo. One of them pulled out a cell phone and made a call.

"He's not calling his wife," I said softly to Gonzalo.

"I hope we pass," Gonzalo replied quietly.

"You are Americans?" one of the men asked.

"Yes," I replied. "You have our passports."

"Where do you live in America?"

"Cleveland. In Ohio."

"And you are tourists here? Just the two of you?"

"Yes, we are. We are good friends in Ohio. We wanted our wives to come with us to Bolivia and Peru, but they decided to stay home. So we are traveling together. Just the two of us. This mountainous region is one of the most beautiful places I have ever seen."

"*¿Hablan español?*" one of them, apparently the senior one, asked.

"I do, a little," I replied. That should have been evident as we had been conversing in Spanish, mine deliberately bumbling with common errors. "My friend does not." Gonzalo had remained silent during this interchange.

"What do you do in Ohio?" Not a question that I was really prepared for. And I thought I should not tell him I was a professor interested in doing studies in Bolivia.

"I am a businessman. I own a car dealership. Two of them, in fact. I sell automobiles."

"Oh. What make?"

I was uncertain why these questions were being asked. Part of generally evaluating us, I supposed. I replied. "Chevrolets and GMC trucks at one. Toyotas at the other."

"And this other man here, your friend? What does he do?"

"He has a company that installs and services heating and air conditioning units in homes and small commercial properties." I doubted that the officer understood what that occupation might be, but he seemed to accept it.

Once again, the officer paged through our passports. He handed them back to us. "*Bueno.* You may proceed."

The border stations—Bolivian and Peruvian—were open. There were two trucks ahead of us, and then we found ourselves with the Bolivian emigration officials. We assumed they would have been alerted and, like the men at the road block we had just cleared, would also be looking for two men. We hoped that they had been told these two would be driving a Volkswagen. I rolled down the window and presented our two American passports.

"*¿Americanos?*"

"Yes. *Si.*"

He took our passports, walked into the building, and returned with another agent, evidently a more senior official. "*¿A donde van?*" he asked. I explained in stumbling Spanish that we were tourists visiting South America, that we had rented the car in La Paz, and that we planned to take the train from Puno to Cuzco and then take the train to Machu Picchu before returning. He asked to see the car rental papers, which Gonzalo retrieved from the glove box and I presented to him. That this examination was necessary after we had just cleared the nearby road block probably had more to do with Bolivian bureaucracy than Bolivian security, I thought.

"Can you suggest a place where we might leave the car?" I asked.

"Not at the railroad station," he said. "It would not be safe there. There are several garages in Puno. Arrange with one of them to keep the car." While talking to us he paged carefully through our passports. He then took the entry forms from them. "You are leaving Bolivia," he said. "You will have to complete new immigration and customs entry forms when you return. Do not bring any food or any drugs."

"*Claro,*" I said.

He waved us on. We then stopped for Peruvian immigration and customs. "Anything to declare?" the official asked.

"*Nada.*"

He saluted us and waved us forward.

I turned to Gonzalo. "We're out of Bolivia. Do you think we'll be followed here—in Peru?"

"Oh, I expect so. Yes, for sure. Of course they can't arrest me here, but with a gun in my back, what could I do?"

We drove north toward Puno. About an hour, we surmised. We were not going to be in time for the nine-o'clock departure of the train to Cuzco. After about a half-hour, I stopped the car, opened the trunk and found a screw driver and a wrench. I removed the license plates, front and rear. One I tossed to the right, as far from the road as I could. Then, after driving another hundred yards, I tossed the other to the left.

Entering Puno, we parked the car at the roadside about one hundred yards from the railroad station. We left the key in the ignition, took the registration and rental documents from the glove box, and walked to the station. Outside we found a teen-aged boy selling cigarettes. Gonzalo bought a cigarette. *"Y un fosforo,"* he said to the boy, asking for a match. Gonzalo then told the boy that he had noticed a car just up the road that had no license plates and that its key was in the ignition. "Someone must have left it there. Maybe in a hurry to catch the train, or something." He pointed to the Datsun. The young man paused, thinking about the situation. He then collected his wares and ambled toward the car. Reaching it, he climbed inside. The car then disappeared up a side street. Gonzalo crumpled the car's documents at the roadside and lit them with the match he had obtained, adding the cigarette to the burning papers. At the station we found that the Cuzco train had left, as we expected. There would not be another train until the following morning.

We found a modest hotel—there were several on the main street of Puno—and secured lodging for the night. Our choice was the Hotel Real. We registered, booking a double room and presenting our passports to the clerk. "We're tourists—Americans—on our way to Cuzco and Arequipa. We'll not be going back to Bolivia. Can you change our Bolivian *bolivianos* into *soles?*"

"I should be able to do that, but I won't be able to give you the bank rate. But there isn't a bank here, anyway. There's a *cambio* at the station, but it won't be open until just before the train leaves. And their rate is the same as ours."

"Okay," I said, as Gonzalo and I emptied our pockets of our Bolivian money. We collected the Peruvian *soles*, our passports, and our room key, then climbed the stairs to the second floor and found our room.

"Well," I said, "there is not much regal about this hotel, despite its name. Now then, we have to find a way to spend today mostly out of sight. I hope that doesn't mean sitting in this dreary hotel all day."

"You know," Gonzalo said, "the Uru people live on floating reed islands in the lake here. I've never seen them, but I bet there are tourist boats that would take us out onto the lake to see their islands."

"Sounds interesting—and out of the way," I replied. "Grab your pack and let's go."

"No point in taking our packs," Gonzalo said.

"But we should, always," I replied. "Hard to predict what will happen. The Boy Scout motto is 'Be Prepared.' That should be ours as well on this junket. Who knows? Maybe we won't come back here."

"Okay. You're right."

We left our room key at the hotel desk and made our way to the waterfront, where we booked a tour to the Uru reed-island settlements that would keep us away from any pursuers for several hours. And it proved to be fascinating. On the boat we were told by a man who was apparently some sort of tour guide that there were seventy islands, all of them made of reeds and floating on the water. These settlements, he told us, date to pre-Incan times. More than that, little was known about the origins of the Uru people. We would, of course, visit the most important, the most typical of these island communities. And, I thought to myself, the one that gives the largest kick-back to our guide on souvenir sales. We pulled up to one of the islands that appeared to house a modest-sized community. At the point where we stopped, booths had been set up and souvenirs were being offered for sale. Made on the island, I wondered, or imported from China? We did not succumb to the lure of these items; several of our fellow passengers on the tour boat did.

Returning to the dock at Puno, we found one of the ANSEB agents waiting for us on the dock. As we pulled in, I said to Gonzalo, "I think he is the guy you pushed into the drink at Copacabana." As we left the boat, he collared Gonzalo, moving him to the side so that other passengers could disembark. He berated Gonzalo and waved his gun, again trying to arrest him or somehow force him to return to La Paz in his custody. My turn, I thought, and I rushed across the dock to push him into the lake.

"Let's go," shouted Gonzalo, and we took off running. Then, "Follow me." We ran back to the railroad station, where we again found the boy selling cigarettes, the boy to whom we had given the car.

"Listen, my friend," Gonzalo said as he passed a one-hundred-*sol* note to the boy. "We need your help. But I can't tell you here. We need to get out of sight. Then I can explain." The boy took the money, quickly picked up his cigarettes and led us hurriedly up the side street where he had previously taken the car.

"I am a Bolivian," Gonzalo began. "I am a businessman. I have a used car business. My friend here works for me there. I also have sort of gotten involved in Bolivian politics. That is, I campaigned against Morales in the elections. *Campesinos* elected Morales; business people campaigned against him. I have continued to speak out against him, but I am not a criminal and not dishonest. I've done nothing wrong except speak out against Morales. Now he has shut down my auto business and is trying to arrest me. So we—I and my salesman friend—are on the run. His agents have just found us. We need to hide."

The boy seemed thoughtful. Then he said, "Come." He led us two blocks further along the street. The houses became smaller, I observed. He stopped at one and said, "I live here, with my mother."

A woman appeared at the door. "Jaime, what's all this?"

Gonzalo stepped forward and repeated what he had told the boy. "Can you hide us?" he asked. "We can pay you."

Jaime's mother seemed thoughtful. Then she led us around the house to a shed. "You can hide there tonight, but you must leave in the morning. There is some straw you can sleep on."

"Many thanks," Gonzalo said.

"Two hundred *soles*," she stated. I peeled off two one-hundred *sol* notes and gave them to her.

"Is there a place nearby, out of the way, where we can get some supper?"

"In the next street, right through that alley. There is a bar that serves some food."

At dinner that night we ate hamburgers. Once again we failed to find the *trucha* that we had been unable to finish in Copacabana. We returned to the shed after our supper.

"Nobody should bother us here," I commented to Gonzalo.

"Yes, but...."

26

WE STUMBLED AWAKE in the morning, stiff but ready for breakfast. We found Jaime's mother and said goodbye, offering profuse thanks to the woman who had sheltered us. She had a question for us. "How much do you think I can get for the car you gave to Jaime? We have no use for it, and money is always welcome. I am a widow. My husband worked on a road crew, but that didn't pay much—barely enough for food and Jaime's school fees. He was killed a year ago when a speeding truck hit him. A lawyer tried to get me some money from the truck driver, but he didn't. I guess the driver was just as poor as we are."

"Well, the car's in good mechanical shape, although the body is a bit battered," Gonzalo replied. "And you don't have registration papers for it. It came from my second-hand car lot. Because the body has some dents and scratches, I have not been able to sell it. That's why I gave it to Jaime." Whether or not she believed

Gonzalo, she did not question the car's origins further nor ask why we chose to get rid of it. "In La Paz it is probably worth about twenty thousand *bolivianos*—with its papers," Gonzalo continued. "I would ask thirty, but bargain down to twenty. *Bolivianos* and *soles* are about the same. Is there a car dealership here in Puno? If so, you could do a little comparative shopping—a little snooping—to see what a similar car might be priced at."

"No, not here in Puno."

"Well then, I suggest you ask about twenty-five thousand *soles* and be prepared to come down to fifteen. Don't bargain too hard, or you might find yourself trying to explain your possession of a car without papers. Find a notary or someone who can type out a respectable-looking bill of sale for you."

"Many thanks. You have given us so much. I wish I could do more to repay you."

"But you have helped us," I said. "Jaime especially. So we thank you." I wondered if the car's absence of VIN numbers might impede a sale of the car. Probably would not be noticed, I supposed. Or, if noticed, ignored.

We made our way back to the Hotel Real. A buffet was laid out for hotel guests. We gave the server the number of the room we had signed in for but not occupied and enjoyed a hearty breakfast. American rather than Bolivian, probably because most of the hotel guests were North American tourists.

"Look," Gonzalo said. "There's Jaime out at his place hoping to sell cigarettes."

"You know, we need tickets for the train. Let's see if he can get them for us." I went to the door, put my fingers to my lips, and gave a loud whistle. Jaime looked our way, and I waved him to us.

"Jaime, my man, you've been very helpful to us. Would you do us another favor? If you will buy us two first-class tickets on this morning's train to Cuzco, we'll give you another tip." I peeled off ten one-hundred *sol* notes and handed them to him. That should cover it, I thought. Jaime took the money and ran to the station. Shortly he returned with our tickets. He handed us our change, and I gave him one hundred *soles*.

"Thank you, thank you very much," he said. "I hope you have a good trip to Cuzco."

"Yes, we will." But first of all, a good trip to Cuzco meant getting on the train, hopefully leaving the ANSEB men behind.

"I wonder," I said to Gonzalo, "where our followers spent the night."

"Not our problem."

We sat in the dining room of the Hotel Real until ten minutes before the scheduled train departure time. Then we hurried across the road to board the train. Not surprisingly, two ANSEB agents were waiting to greet us beside the train. One of them reached out and took hold of Gonzalo's arm. "Gonzalo Mamani, you are under arrest for treason."

Gonzalo shook him off. "Nonsense. I am an American. Let go of me." I pushed between them, and Gonzalo climbed into the first class coach. I followed.

"Well," I commented, "I think we can count on their company all the way to Cuzco."

27

TICKETS IN HAND, we settled into the first-class coach. There were many empty seats; we chose a pair from which we could look out to see the station platform. We briefly investigated the regular coach behind us. It was crowded. We were glad we had the money to pay for the first class tickets. Good use of the *soles* we had been given.

Departure time arrived, but the train did not move. Passengers were still climbing aboard and crowding into the regular fare coaches. About a half-hour behind schedule, the train started to move. Out the window we saw two men run and catch the train, climbing into the economy coach behind us.

"There they are," I said to Gonzalo. "They're going with us."

"Yes, but I don't think they can do much to us during the train trip. They can't arrest me here. They could force us off the train, but then where would we and they be? There would be no way back until another train, and that would be late in the day—maybe this same train heading back tomorrow. And they would have a tough time hanging on to us, I think."

As the crow flies, or maybe the condor might fly if it were on the Altiplano, Puno to Cuzco is about 150 miles. Our train would cover this distance in about eight hours, arriving about two and one-half hours after the schedule alleged it would. Along the way, it would make more than two dozen stops. This train was the link with the world for many Peruvian Altiplano hamlets.

Somewhat after midday, we descended from the train at one of the stops to buy lunch from one of the many vendors that crowded every stopping place. We chose cooked items and beer—safe to eat and drink anywhere. *Salteñas*—my favorite and, I thought, maybe my last opportunity to have them—for me. Something broiled on a skewer for Gonzalo. Women selling knit goods crowded around us. I wished I could buy a poncho for Susan, but I doubted that I could get it to Salaverry and wherever I might go after that. The two men we assumed were ANSEB agents got off the train at our lunch stop. They watched us, but purchased nothing. Don't they have some sort of expense money for lunch, I wondered.

I was making my way through the crowd of hustlers selling food and local wares and generally moving toward the train, when I glanced back to see Gonzalo up against a building wall, hands in the air, with one of the ANSEB man pointing a gun at him. Without really thinking but knowing that I had to do something, I ran toward them. I screamed liked a banshee. People turned and looked at me. I have never been a fighter—not even a grade school playground scrapper—but I assumed my best Muhammad Ali persona and swung my fist into the agent's abdomen. He doubled over. I grabbed his arm, swinging it away from Gonzalo. The gun fired, sending a bullet into the ground. I wrested the gun from him and threw it as hard as I could. It sailed over the train.

People scattered, hurrying away from the mad scene. Gonzalo ran to the train, and I followed. On the train, we looked out the window to see the two ANSEB men climb into the coach behind us just as the train was beginning to move. "Well," I said to Gonzalo, "I guess we provided some excitement for this little town today."

With that bit of excitement behind us, we decided to remain on the train at future stops. At one stop we watched a Peruvian woman trying to sell a knit poncho to those of us in the first class car—obviously the more affluent passengers and probably mostly tourists who might buy her wares. She had her eyes fixed on a woman in the seat just ahead of us. The passenger woman had been passing time during the long journey knitting something, perhaps a sweater, I thought, using a circular needle. Then I observed the woman, the passenger, gesturing with her hands. The Peruvian woman was similarly gesturing.

As the train slowly got under way, I asked the woman passenger what had been transpiring. "The woman wanted my circular needle, and offered to trade a lovely poncho for it. But I have a sweater for my son-in-law half-finished on it. Otherwise I might have given it up."

"But the gesturing, your hands?"

"American sign language. I'm a speech therapist back in Omaha. She must be deaf. I wonder how she learned signing."

"So what did she say? Is that the right word? Or sign?"

"That's beautiful."

"Amazing," I commented. "She doesn't speak English. You don't speak Spanish—or Quechua—and yet you two could communicate. There's something nice about that."

Not long after our lunch stop, one of the ANSEB men came from the coach behind into our car. He came up to our seat and leaned over to Gonzalo, who was sitting next to me in the window seat, and launched into a verbal tirade that was too rapid for me to understand. Gonzalo put out hands, palms up, and shook his head. *"No hablo español,"* he said in an American accent. "I am American and speak only English. I don't speak Spanish." The ANSEB agent grabbed Gonzalo's arm and continued his tirade.

I stood up, shoved the ANSEB man aside, and waved to the conductor who was at the front of the car. He strode quickly to our seats. *"¿Que pasa?"*

"Somos Americanos, touristas," I said. Then, changing into English and hoping to be understood but not wanting to reveal my Spanish fluency, "We don't know what this man wants. He is attacking my friend, who does not speak any Spanish."

"Stand aside," the conductor commanded the agent, pushing him to the other side of the aisle. Then to us, "May I see your passports, please?" He examined our American passports and turned to the ANSEB agent. "Your ticket, please." One glance at the agent's ticket and then, "You have a coach ticket. This is a first-class car. Return to your car and stay there. If you come here again, I will stop the train and put you off—wherever we are at the moment."

"But they are Bolivian criminals," the ANSEB agent said.

"With American passports? Not likely." We were glad that the conductor seemed sympathetic to us. "Return to your seat in the rear coach, now."

In halting Spanish mixed with English, I thanked the conductor profusely. Gonzalo added his thanks, in English. *"Un boracho, tal vez,"* commented the conductor.

I translated for Gonzalo, "A drunkard, perhaps."

But the ANSEB agent was not so easily deterred. About twenty minutes later he was back. The conductor saw him and hurried to our rescue. "I told you to stay in the coach car," he said.

"This man is a dangerous, violent criminal. He is wanted in Bolivia. It is my duty to arrest him."

"Not here," said the conductor. "This is Peru, and these men have American passports. They are not Bolivians." With that he grabbed the agent's arm. "I warned you. You are off this train." The train was, in fact, slowing to a stop at another village. The conductor led the agent to the rear of our car and forced him off the train. But he was not gone. Looking back from the window I watched him reenter the coach behind us as the train slowly resumed its journey.

The sun was far in the west as the panoramic spread of red
tile roofs of Cuzco appeared. The train made a series of dramatic
switch-backs and took us down into Cuzco.

28

WE SAT IN OUR SEATS, watching as disembarking passengers made their way along the platform to the terminal building.
We saw the ANSEB agents leave, one at the head of the crowd,
the other lingering behind. The conductor approached us. "We
hope to avoid the man who accosted my friend," I said. "He
seems to have reboarded the train, and he is just walking up the
platform now."

"*Bueno,*" he replied. "What you should do is go back to the
last car of the train. Then get off and walk back along the platform to a bridge that crosses to the next platform. The train from
Machu Picchu is due to arrive on that platform in about fifteen
minutes. There will be many passengers leaving that train. Join
the crowd, and you should be able to leave the station unseen."

"*Gracias, muchisimas gracias,*" I thanked the conductor.

We followed the conductor's advice and soon found ourselves in Cuzco's central plaza. "There's a tourist information
center over there," I said pointing across the plaza. "I have some
thoughts about what we should do next."

"Okay," replied Gonzalo. "What's your master plan?"

"I think," I said, "that we should go into the information
center. While I browse racks for possibly useful folders and schedules, you should go to the desk. In fluent Spanish, you should
explain that we have just arrived by train from Bolivia and need a
place to stay. Tell them we are Bolivians, if you have the chance.
Ask about hotels, good ones, upscale ones, but maybe not the
very best, not the most expensive. If they offer to make a reservation, say 'No, we'd rather look first.' Get a map of Cuzco.
And ask about bus or train travel to Arequipa. Let them think we
are headed there. And about international airport connections in

Arequipa. Arequipa is an interesting place we would like to see, maybe spend a day, but then we will want to fly out, perhaps to Chile or Ecuador. Ask if there are direct flights. Can we avoid Lima? We want to get to Arequipa, but we would like to avoid Lima."

"We're not going to Arequipa, are we?" Gonzalo asked. "It's not on the way to Salaverry."

"No, no, no. We are trying to lay a false trail. That's all. As I browse folders in racks, I'll try to pick up bus schedules to Lima. I think we'll have to go there and then on from there to Trujillo and Salaverry."

"That sounds right to me," Gonzalo commented. "We'll need someplace to stay tonight. Someplace other than one of the hotels they recommend."

"Hopefully, I can find something useful in a brochure while you're at the desk."

Outside the visitor center and carrying a bundle of brochures and tourist information, we ambled across the plaza. The square was ringed with outfitters whose window placards urged tourists to book a hike to Machu Picchu with them. Hiking the old Inca ridge-top trail seemed to be the favored way to reach the old Inca site. Judging by the young people we saw in the plaza, many of the hikers would be German.

There were many shops selling souvenirs. "Look at all the beads," I said to Gonzalo, commenting on the impressive variety of beads offered by street-side vendors. "They are amazing."

"Yes," he replied, "Cuzco is known for its beads."

Looking across the plaza, we saw the two ANSEB agents enter the tourist office. "Okay," I said, "time to get out of here. What did you find out about hotels?"

"I guess I would choose the Hotel Terra Incaica," Gonzalo said. "It's close. Just off the plaza. But we're not going to stay in a hotel."

"No, of course not. But the ANSEB men don't know that."

We registered at the Terra Incaica, showing our passports and once again explaining that we were American tourists. "We'll visit

Machu Picchu and then go to Arequipa," I said. Taking our room key, we went to the attractive double room the hotel had given us.

"Let's mess up the bed and towels. Make this room look used," I said.

Gonzalo then spread out the Cuzco map while I opened a brochure listing guest houses. "It looks like there are a couple of possible places two or three blocks down the next street."

"Okay, let's check them out." We left the hotel, dropping the key at the desk, and set out to find our accommodations for the night.

We chose the second of the guest houses we encountered. We were welcomed by a friendly, middle-aged woman who greeted us and offered us coca tea. "It will help with the altitude sickness," she said, pouring the green tea into cups. "The hotels offer oxygen, but that only delays the symptoms. Coca tea is the best thing to take."

As we sipped the coca tea, I told our hostess that we had just flown from Lima. And I told her that LAN had left our luggage behind. We had only the small packs we had carried on. "They promise the rest of it tomorrow," I added.

"Yes," she said, "I know. It is often like that. LAN is our national airlines, and it is a disgrace. It is always late, and luggage is often left behind. They will tell you it's because of the altitude, but that is nonsense. Planes fly much higher than Cuzco."

"We were an hour late leaving Lima," I commented. "No reason why, that we were told."

"Of course," she said. "It is always like that. Practically every day."

I told our hostess we would spend the next day in Cuzco and take the morning train to Machu Picchu the following day. We would return to her place the subsequent day after a night in Machu Picchu. We booked a room for three nights, and I paid her for three nights, I told her I would pay for subsequent nights when we returned. "We plan to be in Cuzco for two or three additional days before going to Arequipa," I said.

"The train is really the best way to go to Machu Picchu," she said. "It's a beautiful ride along the Urubamba River. There are buses," she said, "cheaper, but I don't recommend them."

"We are looking forward to the train ride. I have read about it."

"Machu Picchu is a wonderful place. Magical," she said. "It's lower than Cuzco. You won't have altitude problems there, I think. Be sure to see the sundial. Well, it's not really a sundial. It's the upright stone where the Inca priests hitched the sun so they could call it back after the solstice."

"Winter or summer solstice?" I wondered aloud. "Maybe both," I continued, musing. "We're not far from the equator. You know, I have actually stood on the equator. Twice, in fact. Once in Ecuador and once in Uganda." Then, again to our hostess, I asked, "Should we climb Huayna Picchu, the mountain? I have heard that it offers spectacular views."

"No. That is a very difficult, almost impossible trail up a very steep mountain. It is for people much younger than you. There is lots else to see."

Changing the subject, I asked about places in Cuzco to eat. "You shouldn't eat much until you are adjusted to the altitude," she warned.

"Yes, but we need something," I responded. "Is there not a quiet place near here where we can get a light supper?"

"*Claro*," she said. "But do not go back to the plaza or any of the hotels there. They would serve you too much and charge you a lot. Just down the street in the next block there is a small, neighborhood restaurant. Eat there—but just a little! And no alcohol—no wine, no beer!"

Upstairs in our room, Gonzalo asked, "Why did you pay for three nights? We're not going to Machu Picchu."

"Will ANSEB find her?" I asked. "Probably not. But if they do, I don't want her to know our real plans or to think of us as anything other than two American tourists."

"Right. Of course. Somehow I keep forgetting who we are!"

"And maybe we should go to Machu Picchu. I think we have time."

We spread out the brochures we had acquired and began going through them. "Look at this," I said. "There are Tepsa buses to Lima leaving every few hours. It looks like it takes about twenty hours to reach Lima. How are you at sleeping on a bus?"

"Better than sleeping in a Bolivian jail!" Gonzalo replied. "Let's do it."

29

AFTER BREAKFAST, we walked to the central plaza. Cuzco's cathedral was erected atop an Inca temple. Many of the temple's stones were used in building the cathedral, and the foundations and lower walls of the cathedral walls simply incorporated preexisting temple stone-work. We stopped in a street that ran along the side of the cathedral and admired the amazing remnants of Inca walls. Working without tempered metals for tools and without mortar, the early stone masons had cut and fitted together enormous blocks of granite, so closely positioned that a piece of paper could not be inserted between them. I was impressed.

"Look," Gonzalo said as he clutched my arm and pointed down the street to the plaza. "There they are." Two of the now familiar ANSEB agents were in the plaza, walking slowly and scanning the surrounding buildings. They seemed to be most interested in hotel entrances. They talked to a doorman at one of the hotels. One of them entered the hotel.

"Quick," I said. I grabbed Gonzalo's arm and hastily steered him into the cathedral."

But a short minute later, the two ANSEB agents followed us into the sanctuary.

"Over here," Gonzalo said as he led me to a confessional at the side of the sanctuary. As he entered the priest's side and pulled the dark curtain around him, he said to me, "Kneel there. You are a penitent asking forgiveness." I knelt at the penitent's place as directed.

"Father, I have sinned," I said in a low voice. "I have sheltered and aided a dangerous criminal. I have helped him escape."

"You are forgiven," Gonzalo responded. Then I started on a litany of imagined sins that made it difficult for Gonzalo not to laugh.

Our two ANSEB followers walked past us without giving attention to us, apparently not suspecting us. They left through a side door.

Abandoning the confessional, we found seats in a dark corner. "We need a plan. We need to figure out how to spend today without being caught."

"I think," Gonzalo began.

"Good," I interrupted. "We really do need some heavy-duty thinking! We have a major problem."

"Listen, my friend," Gonzalo said. "This is a tourist place. There's a lot to see in the neighborhood. We should do some big-time sight-seeing. Let's find a tourist agency and book a tour for the day, not here, but at some of the nearby tourist places. Places that will get us out of town."

"Yeah, okay, good," I responded.

"I noticed a Lima Tours office practically next door to the cathedral," Gonzalo commented. "Let's become American tourists again and see what they can do for us."

The staff at Lima Tours was eager to help two probably well-heeled American tourists. "I speak only a little Spanish," I said to a man at a desk, "and Mr. Morrison speaks none. We'll need an English-speaking guide."

"No problem. Not a problem at all."

"It's now what—about ten in the morning. We have most of the day, but we have to be back here for an important meeting at four this afternoon. Perhaps we should be back about three-thirty." I invented this meeting, for I wanted to be back in good time to figure out what we might be able to do about dinner without ANSEB. The local café again, perhaps.

"No problem. Not a problem at all. When do you want to leave? Where would you like to go? What would you like to see?"

"Well," Gonzalo said, "we can leave now—or as soon as you can find a guide who speaks English. And we have only arrived yesterday. So you should tell us what to see."

"We are going to Machu Picchu tomorrow," I added, "and then we will go next to Arequipa."

"Very good." Then he turned his head and called, "Eduardo, Edward."

A young man—about thirty, I guessed—came from a back room carrying a cup of coffee. "These two American gentlemen would like a tour, returning here by three-thirty. What would you think of Písac and Sacsaywaman?"

"Well, it's Friday, so there won't be too much activity at the Písac market. But the ruins there are interesting. And there are places to get lunch in Písac, if we were to leave now. It's about a forty-five minute drive, maybe only half an hour since today is not a market day. Then after lunch, Sacsaywaman. The immense red granite ruins there are well worth a visit."

With a driver and English-speaking Edward, we were soon under way. Out of the reach of ANSEB for the day, we hoped. "We're still going to have to figure out how to handle the bus station," Gonzalo whispered into my ear.

"For now, let's relax and enjoy being tourists," I whispered back.

And so we did. The ruins at Písac were awesome. The land was terraced, and structures had been erected upon the terraces. As we had been at the cathedral in Cuzco, we were impressed by the stone work with carved blocks tightly abutting one another. "But you will be even more impressed when you visit Machu Picchu," Edward told us.

After about an hour at Písac, we drove to Sacsaywaman. We were awed. Gigantic stones formed the wall of what seemed to be a fortress. "Yes," said Edward, "it does seem to be a fortress. But the archeologists are not sure about that. Actually, its origins are pretty much unknown. It goes back to before Incan times. However, it was used as a military post by the Incas."

Ambling along beside the gigantic rock face of the fortress

or whatever it was, I suddenly saw a man who I thought might be one of the ANSEB agents. I pointed him out to Gonzalo. "Is that who I think it is?"

"Maybe, I'm not sure. Well, probably."

I walked over to Edward. "Amazing," I said. "I guess we might go on back now."

"Okay, if you've seen enough."

We climbed into the Lima Tours car. As we did, I noticed the ANSEB man running toward us.

30

"WE HAVE TOLD EVERYONE we are going to Machu Picchu," I said to Gonzalos. "I think we should do it. We've been moving right along, and we have a day to spare. I'd rather spend it in Machu Picchu than Salaverry."

"I'm for it," said my friend. "Have you been there?

"No. Have you?"

"Once long ago, when I was a university student. With some other students."

"Can we spend the whole day there?' I asked.

"Not so simple," Gonzalo replied, "at least as I understand it. The return buses to catch the train leave from the ruins by about three o'clock."

"Hmm."

"But I have an idea," Gonzalo offered. "Campers hike in there. They must sleep somewhere. Not in the ruins, but back on the trail, I suppose. Let's buy sleeping bags at one of the outfitting stores here and plan to spend the night on the trail. Shouldn't be much worse than Señor Quispe's barn." We stopped at an outfitting store on a corner of the plaza, one of many such emporiums. "Let me see what I can find for sleeping bags," Gonzalo said, and he entered the store. I stood outside, the ever-watchful sentry. Then, almost suddenly, one of the ANSEB men came around the corner and took hold of my arm.

"Who are you? What are you doing here? How are you connected to Mamani? Don't you know he's a dangerous man, a criminal?"

I shook him off and started walking across the plaza away from the store and Gonzalo. "And who are you?" I asked angrily. "Leave me alone."

"I am a Bolivian security agent. We're tracking a dangerous criminal. I've seen him with you. In Copacabana, in Puno, now here."

"Nonsense. I'm an American. I don't know what you are talking about. Leave me alone." I walked on across the plaza, heading toward the city hall, where I assumed I could find a Peruvian police officer. He let go of my arm, obviously a bit concerned as we neared a point where he might have to justify himself. Then, unable to restrain myself, I taunted, *"Vete a friar monos"* (Go fry monkeys), a schoolyard put-down my kids had learned during our year living in La Paz. I walked into the city hall. He did not follow me.

I wanted to reconnect with Gonzalo, but I did not want to lead the ANSEB man to him or to the boarding house where we were staying. So I walked along the side of the plaza and entered the Terra Incaica. As I hoped it would, the hotel had a street level café just off of its lobby. I picked up a newspaper from a rack in the lobby, went in to the café, and ordered coffee. I watched the ANSEB agent as he entered the hotel and talked to the clerk at the reception desk. Another hotel man came from a back office, perhaps a manager, I thought. The manager went back into the office and returned with what I supposed was a registry of guests. He and the ANSEB agent went through it carefully, line by line. The agent pointed to me. The manager nodded. I sipped my coffee and read the newspaper. The agent left the hotel—to wait outside, I presumed.

Leaving the hotel, I wandered about the plaza, looking into shops. I bought some beads. Susan would like them, if I could get them back with me. Somehow I had to lose the agent before reconnecting with Gonzalo. I returned to the information office we had visited when we first arrived in Cuzco. Keeping my eye on my follower, I browsed through pamphlets. I talked to the person at the desk about the best way to go to Machu Picchu. Buses or the train, which I already knew. No, they did not need to book the train for me, but many thanks. I picked up a map of the city and plotted out a side-street route back to the boarding house. Finally—it seemed forever to me—the ANSEB man wandered back into the plaza and out of direct sight of the office entrance. I hurried out, turned away from the plaza, and made my way back to our lodging.

I admired the bags Gonzalo had purchased. "But," I said, "I think we need to buy some more things. I've been in this same shirt and pants for what seems like forever. Sleeping in them sometimes—in the straw, on the ground. I think it's time to buy some new clothes."

"Absolutely," Gonzalo replied. "Let's go do it." And so we did, managing not to become entangled with the ANSEB agents. I bought khaki pants with lots of pockets, including a couple of inner ones with zippers. All the money I was carrying would probably be safe there. Gonzalo bought Levis. We both purchased new shirts. We also purchased underwear. We felt no need to burden ourselves with washing out underwear when we could afford to buy new and clean.

"I suppose we could see if the woman at the guest house would wash the old clothes for us," Gonzalo said.

"Not mine," I said. "I never want to see them again. Besides, our small packs have no extra room. Out with the old!"

"Right."

31

THE NEXT MORNING found us boarding the train with our small packs and newly acquired sleeping bags to descend down the valley of the Urubamba River to Aguas Calientes. It was a spectacular trip. Steep cliffs rose up on each side, cradling the tumbling, cascading river.

Off the train, we joined a line waiting for one of the jitney buses to take us up about 1,000 feet to Machu Picchu. "No wonder it is called the 'lost city of the Incas,'" I said to Gonzalo. "Even knowing that it's there, it really disappears into the mountain."

"Well, that's because it is native stone buildings set on native stone. The Spaniards came down this river valley without ever finding the Incas above them."

We were on one of the last buses to climb the twisting road up. Partway up, the driver stopped the bus and got out. Now what, I thought. Shortly he returned with a handful of wild orchids. Beautiful. Graciously and with a modest bow, he presented them to an attractive young woman seated beside a man of about her age. A honeymoon couple, I thought. And so, perhaps, did the bus driver.

Descending from the bus, we paid our entrance fee and presented our American passports. There were many guides, huckstering and enrolling tourists in groups. We decided to tour the ruins on our own. The pamphlet we were handed at the entrance had a map.

I overheard one of the guides talking about the "sacred site." In fact, in Cuzco I had seen and heard repeated reference to the "sacred lost city" of the Incas and the "sacred valley" of the Urubamba River. Being a cynic—part of being a scientist—I was certain that no one really knew that Machu Picchu was a sacred site. In fact, I recalled reading that those who lived there and why they did so remained a mystery to archeologists despite many efforts to find clues. As for being lost, it certainly had not been lost to the Incans who lived there. And Hiram Bingham found it by paying a local boy to guide him, for it was known to local residents if not to adventurers from Yale. Yet, both "sacred" and "lost" were descriptors that promoters of tourism found useful. I knew and understood that Peru's economy could use all the foreign tourist currency it could entrap.

A buffet lunch had been set up at the small hotel next to the ruins, and we took advantage of it much earlier than we would usually have eaten, assuming that long lines would develop.

Standing in a lunch line did not seem to us to be a profitable way to pass our limited time at Machu Picchu.

Back in the ruins I realized Gonzalo was no longer with me. Oh well, I thought, we'll find each other as the crowds depart. I wandered through the ancient city. If the stone work at the cathedral in Cuzco had been impressive, so much more so was this, I thought to myself. Enormous lintels; how did they ever get them in place? For that matter, how did these amazing builders cut these many stone blocks so precisely with no metal other than gold, silver, and copper? Soft metals. No steel. What were their tools?

I saw the young couple from the bus standing near the erect stone said to be a sundial. They were holding hands. She still had the flowers.

Then, in the older and less elaborate section of the ruins, I saw Gonzalo. He was standing near the edge of the mountain with its steep drop-off. The agent from ANSEB was there with him. The same one we had baptized in Lake Titicaca—twice. How did he get here? Gonzalo was gesticulating and speaking in English. A crowd was beginning to gather.

I strode to the agent, grabbed his arm, and spun him around. "Listen to me. I don't know who you are or why you are bothering us on our vacation. But if you don't leave us alone, I'll push you off the edge here. It's not as wet as Lake Titicaca, but it's a lot farther down."

He looked at me, glaring, not friendly. There was little he could do at this place, and English-speaking tourists were rapidly surrounding us. "I'll be with you on the train back to Cuzco," he said. "My colleagues will meet the train, and then we'll get you and take you back to Bolivia."

"We're not going back to Bolivia. Not now. And after you and all you've done following us, never. Never, ever. We're going on to Arequipa, and we do not want to see you there." He left, grumbling to himself. Too large a crowd had gathered for him to be able to do anything else.

"Well, Gonzalo, the minute you leave my side you get in

trouble. This can't happen again. You have to stay with me; we have to stay together."

Gonzalo clearly was annoyed. "You know, Paul, I'm a big boy. And I know my way around South America better than you do. Get off my case!"

"No, Gonzalo, being 'on your case' is what I am here for. We stay together. More than that, I call the shots."

"Screw it! Screw you! I'm not an idiot and I'm not helpless."

"Okay, okay, okay. Calm down. We're in this together now. But we're both much safer if we're together, not alone."

"Yeah, you're right," Gonzalo acknowledged reluctantly. "And, while I was off and out from under your watchful eyes, I did some good things."

"Oh?"

"We're booked into the hotel here for the night."

"How in the world did you do that?"

"Well, I offered to pay double, and in cash. You still have plenty of *soles*, don't you? The extra tab will go into his pocket, of course. I hope he really did have the spare room he said he had. I would hate to see someone else displaced. And I offered to give him our sleeping bags, which he should be able to sell. So let's go now and pick up our keys and claim our room. *Trucha* is on the dinner menu for tonight, but it won't be very fresh."

The young couple from the bus and the sundial stone was in the dining room at dinner, seated at a table by themselves.

32

WE BOARDED THE TRAIN to return to Cuzco. Once again we marveled at the Urubamba River Valley. The train traveled slowly; it was uphill all the way.

"Well," I said to Gonzalo, "that was marvelous. I'm glad we fit it in. But now we have some planning to do."

"Yeah," Gonzalo agreed. "They'll be waiting for us at the station."

"I have an idea. See what you think of it."

"Whatever your idea is, it's better than mine. I can't figure out how we'll escape them, and I'm getting more and more worried."

"I guess 'worried' is appropriate."

"Actually, I'm more than worried. I'm terrified!"

"So this I what I suggest," I continued. "When we arrive, I'll head into the station along with the crowd. You go back to the bridge to the other platform. Hang out for a while—fifteen, twenty minutes or however long until the crowd has gone. The ANSEB men will recognize me and try to get me to lead them to you. I'll brush them off, but I'll lead them away and back toward the Hotel Terra Incaica, where we're not really staying but they think we are."

"Sounds good," Gonzalo said. "And I'll meet you back at our room."

"Yeah."

As planned, I disembarked with the crowd of returning tourists. And as expected, I was greeted by one of the ANSEB agents as I left the platform. He took hold of my arm. "Where is he? Where is Mamani? We know you're traveling with him." I ignored him, walking on toward the hotel. But he persisted. "I don't know who you are, but your companion, Mamani, is a dangerous man and he should be in our custody."

"Let go of me!" I said. "I've told you before, I am an American. So is my friend. We're tourists. I have no idea who Mamani is or what you're talking about. Now leave me alone."

"Where is he?" he persisted.

"In Machu Picchu," I said. "He's staying there another day. But he is not whoever you think he is. We're both Americans, from Ohio. Just tourists. So leave us alone."

I walked into the Terra Incaica Hotel and asked the desk clerk if there were any messages. None, of course. Then, seeming to hesitate and be making up my mind, I turned out back to the plaza. I strolled a bit, looking in windows. The ANSEB men seemed to lose interest in me, and I seized the opportunity to turn down a side street and make my way back to the boarding house.

I greeted Gonzalo. "I guess we'll have to spend another night here before going on to Lima. But we should still make Salaverry on schedule. At least I think so. Let's get dinner at the Terra Incaica. Somehow they seem reluctant to try to drag us out of there forcibly."

"Yeah. When it comes down to it, they really have no authority here. They probably expect to put a gun in my back and encourage me to behave that way. But they don't know what to do with you, and that screws up their plans."

"Right. So let's go get dinner. If we catch a bus around midday tomorrow, we should be in Lima in the morning. It's about a twenty hour ride, I believe. At least that's what I can tell from the schedules we picked up."

33

WITH HEADS FULL OF MEMORIES of Machu Picchu, a fantastic and magical place for both of us, we were less than fully excited about spending the morning in Cuzco. Yet we had the morning open, and we wanted to do something that would take us out of view of our followers. Without revealing our departure plans, we interrupted our hostess as she was serving breakfast to ask her about places to visit in Cuzco. "Maybe there are things that most tourists don't see—but should," I said.

"Of course," she replied. She paused, perhaps thinking of alternatives, and then said, "I suggest you visit the Andean Textile Center. There is a small museum there with some exquisite pieces, and you can see weavers at work. You know, weaving goes back thousands of years here."

"Yes," I replied, "my wife is an artist. She paints; she doesn't weave. But she understands and loves art of all kinds. She has taken me to see some weaving exhibits. Before we left, she told me I should be sure to see Andean textiles." I did not add that she had purchased some excellent examples during our year in Bolivia. "Let's go there this morning," I said, turning to Gonzalo.

With new clothes on our backs and with old clothes left in our room, we set out. The museum was worth the visit, and it provided a peaceful refuge from ANSEB. In a quiet corner, I commented to my friend, "You know, Gonzalo, Susan became very interested in the artistry of Andean textiles when we lived here. Amazing, fine work. Some of it done on a back-strap loom. That's nothing more than a warp wound between two poles, one attached to a tree, the other to a strap around the weaver's waist. She, the weaver, can vary the tension by leaning back. And we've seen weaving being done on a warp wound between two poles staked to the ground. Awesome!"

"One of the many extraordinary achievements of my ancestors. Some intricately woven funereal fragments dating back more than a thousand years have been recovered from mummies in Andean graves. I'll have to go to a museum to see such things now, I guess."

"Some that Susan collected you can see in our house in Cleveland Heights. Probably as much there as you can find in most American museums."

"Interestingly, not all of the weaving is done by women," Gonzalo continued. "Rugs and the packing sacks used for the backs of llamas are woven by men."

"Right. I know that."

Leaving the textile center, we went to the Terra Incaica Hotel, hoping to enjoy a leisurely lunch in the hotel café. We had ordered and our food had arrived at our table when two uniformed Peruvian police officers walked to our table. They were accompanied by the hotel manager and the ANSEB man who had most frequently harassed us in the Cuzco plaza. *"Buenas tardes, Señores,"* one of the officers said. "Could I trouble you for your passports, please?" We retrieved our passports from our pockets and presented them to the officer. "You have been to Bolivia?" We continued the fiction that Gonzalo did not speak Spanish, and the officer addressed his question to me.

"Yes," I replied. "We spent several days there."

"And what did you do in Bolivia, Señor Masterson?" He

thumbed through the pages of my passport, checking the border crossing stamps.

"The usual tourist things. I guess. We stayed at the Hotel Europa. We rested for a couple of days to adjust to the altitude. We went to the witches' market on Calle Sagarnaga. We rented a car and drove out to Copacabana and to Tiahuanacu. Then we drove to Puno, where we left the car with a garage. We are going to Arequipa. We'll recover the car and return it when we go back to La Paz."

"What sort of car, please?"

"An ordinary one, a sedan."

"A Volkswagen?

"No, a Datsun."

"And here in Cuzco? You are staying at this hotel?"

The manager spoke up. "Yes, they are."

"And what have you done here in Cuzco?"

"Well, we took a tour with Lima tours to Písac and Saksay-wamon. And we went to Machu Picchu. We spent one night in the hotel there."

The officer turned to the ANSEB man. "They seem to be tourists as they say they are."

"No, they are terrorists, dangerous criminals. I need to arrest them and take them back to Bolivia."

"Their papers are in order. They are Americans, not Bolivians. I suggest you do not further disturb them, or I will arrest you."

"But I am an agent of the Agencia Nacional de la Seguridad de Boliviana."

"And this is el Peru, not Bolivia." He took the ANSEB man by the arm and led him from the hotel.

We resumed our lunch. "That was interesting," Gonzalo commented. "I guess we passed." We continued our lunch, not being sure when we would next have a leisurely meal.

As the scheduled departure time for the Lima bus approached, we walked to the bus station. It was crowded. Buses were waiting to depart to Lima, Arequipa, Puno, and many other destinations. As we were making our way to the departure area, one of the

ANSEB agents appeared. He strode toward us, then took out a hand gun and thrust it into Gonzalo's back. "Gonzalo Mamani, you are under arrest for crimes against the government of Bolivia!"

Gonzalo threw his arms up and screamed out in English, "Help! Help!"

I joined in the cry, "Help, help us! *Ayudanos!*"

A group of six back-packers, three young men and three young women, quickly surrounded us. Probably Americans, I thought. They succeeded in making it impossible for the ANSEB agent to do anything but announce in stentorian tones, "He is a dangerous criminal!"

"I am an American," Gonzalo called out loudly. "I am a tourist. I am not a criminal."

Two uniformed Peruvian police officers arrived within minutes. Two more followed a few minutes later. One of the Peruvian officers caught the ANSEB agent by the wrist and wrested the gun away from him. "He is a dangerous criminal. He is wanted for treason in Bolivia. I am an agent of the government of Bolivia," the ANSEB agent protested as he was led away.

"Now then," said one of the Peruvian officers. "You are Americans?"

"*Si*, yes."

"May I see your passports, please?"

The Peruvian officer looked at our photos in the passports and carefully paged through both of the passports. "*Señor Morrison y Señor Masterson*, where are you going today?" he asked.

"Lima," I replied.

"And what is your business in Lima?"

"Tourism for two days," I replied. "Then we fly home."

"Very good," he said. "That is your bus there."

"Thank you, officer. I really do not know who that man with a gun was."

"We'll take care of him. Have a good trip," he said, and then he walked off.

I turned to the young people who had been standing nearby. "You are Americans, perhaps?"

"Yes," one of them said. "We're taking the bus to Arequipa."

"Thanks so much for coming to our help."

"Glad we could be helpful. The *Lonely Planet* guidebook said to watch out for petty thieves, but not this sort of thing."

"Where are you all from?" I asked.

"Buffalo, and you?"

"Cleveland. We'll be headed home soon, but first we have to get to Lima."

"Have a good trip."

"We will, and many thanks again."

We boarded the bus and soon were on our way to Lima.

34

THE GRAN HOTEL BOLIVAR fronts on Lima's Plaza San Martin, more commonly called the Plaza Mayor. An older hostelry, it has retained its courtly demeanor. High ceilings, dark woodwork, brocade draperies. We checked in, presenting our American passports. "We'll be here for two nights," I said as I tendered the credit card Rosemary had given me. The clerk gave us our room key, a large, old-fashioned key, not a plastic card. "We plan to go to Trujillo," I told the receptionist. "We would rather take a bus or train. We would like to see some of the countryside, rather than simply fly over it. By any chance do you have bus or train schedules?"

"Let me see what I have here," he responded. Presently he produced a bus schedule. "Here, take this. Keep it. No one else will want it. I'm not sure why we have it. Our guests do not generally ride buses." I ignored his denigrating remark. "And here is a tourist map of Central Lima," he added. "The walk from here to the Plaza de Armas goes through the old city and is worth a visit. The best restaurants are in Miraflores. You would have to take a taxi."

"Perhaps tomorrow night. We've traveled a lot today. What of your restaurant here?" I asked.

"It's very good," he replied.

"Do we need to make a dinner reservation?"

"No, no. Not for tonight. Only on a major holiday, perhaps. Probably not even then. Miraflores has stolen most of our dining room business."

I thanked him for the map and the bus schedule, and we made our way to our second-floor room. Throwing our packs on a luggage rack, we sat down in comfortable arm chairs. "This is luxury," Gonzalo commented. "I haven't been this comfortable since leaving La Paz."

"Don't get to used to it," I said. "We'll soon be back on a bus! But for the moment, we seem to be well set and out of the reach of ANSEB. And since we used the credit card to check in, our CIA friends should know where we are."

"Yes, and Rosa Maria," Gonzalo commented.

"Okay," I said, spreading out the bus schedule. "There's a bus to Trujillo leaving at nine this evening. Arrives in Trujillo at six tomorrow morning."

"Great," said Gonzalo. "Another night on a bus."

"We need to keep moving," I replied.

"Yes, yes. So how about we go out and walk up to Plaza de Armas. We can get something to eat on the way. Then back here for a drink and early meal before checking out and taking a taxi to the bus terminal."

"That all works, Gonzalo," I said, "except I think we should simply disappear from this hotel without checking out."

"Do you really think ANSEB can reach us here?"

"No, but remember that I was hired to escort you safely to the U.S. So we'll leave unannounced."

"Okay, Boss Man," Gonzalo replied.

We strolled the pedestrian walkway to the Plaza de Armas, stopping at a café for a late lunch and wandering into side streets to admire the balconies and architecture of colonial-era houses. There were many people, local Peruvians out for a stroll on a Monday afternoon. Also shoppers; the main pedestrian way seemed to have been taken over by shops, many of them with luxury items. Sad, I thought, for an interesting colonial era district to have been thus modernized. We detoured through a less affluent, crowded neighborhood to visit the Museum of the Inquisition. Architecturally an interesting building with a sordid history.

Returning to the Plaza Mayor and the hotel, Gonzalo led me around the corner and along Avenida Nicolás de Piérola to find ceviche at a sidewalk café. We clicked our beer glasses. "Ceviche is an absolutely mandatory part of Lima," Gonzalo declared.

Back in the Gran Hotel Bolivar, we found seats in the bar located behind and up a short stairway from the reception desk and lobby. We could watch the comings and goings in the lobby—of which there were not many. We both ordered pisco sours. "It pains me to say this," Gonzalo commented, "but Peruvian pisco is much better than that of Bolivia."

"This may be your last," I said. "You'll have trouble finding pisco in America."

We were just starting to eat the bar meals we had ordered, when we saw a uniformed man—a police officer—enter the hotel and approach the reception desk. *"Buenas tardes,"* he said to the man at the reception desk. "I am looking for a pair of Bolivian men who are wanted by the Bolivian National Security Agency. It is thought they might be in Lima." He presented his credentials. "This is a faxed picture of one of them." It was the same picture that agents had had at the road block near Puno, I presumed.

"That's an old picture. It really does not look like me," Gonzalo whispered. "Especially since Rosa Maria got me an American haircut."

"We've had two men check in today—Americans—but neither of them looks like that photo you have."

"You are sure they are Americans?"

"Oh, yes. I saw their passports. I have their passport numbers, if you want them."

"No, not necessary. I really don't know why we are checking hotels for the Bolivians. They wouldn't bother to do such a thing for us. Except, I guess, that one of them is a dangerous criminal."

"Well, if we get anyone suspicious here, I'll certainly call you," the reception clerk added. "The two men who came here today are definitely American, and they seem to be ordinary tourists, not criminals." And with that, the police officer turned and started toward the door. Then he stopped and turned back.

"I think I should take down the passport numbers of the two men who checked in here—Americans, you said. It seems silly, but my boss will give me grief if I don't."

"Fine." He pulled out his register, and the officer wrote down our passport numbers. "They're sitting up there in the bar eating an early meal, if you want to talk with them."

"No. I don't think that's necessary." The officer left, and the desk clerk recovered from under the counter a magazine he had been reading.

We finished and paid for our meal, collected our packs, left the hotel, and found a taxi to take us to the bus terminal.

35

OUR BUS ARRIVED in Trujillo about fifteen minutes ahead of its 6:00 A.M. scheduled time. As bus rides go, I thought as I left the bus, this one was quite comfortable. I even slept—some. In fact, I mused, the overnight ride from Cuzco to Lima had also been comfortable. I had not ridden on many long-distance buses in the States, but those I had sampled had much to gain before matching the two Peruvian buses on which we had ridden.

After coffee and rolls for breakfast, we found a taxi and began negotiations with the driver. "We need to go Salaverry," I said.

"Yes," he replied. "I know it. I often go there to meet American cruise ships. I take the tourists to the ruins at Chan Chan. But there is no cruise ship today. Tomorrow there will be one, I think."

"Well then," Gonzalo said, "you can take us to Salaverry."

"*Claro.*"

"Now then," I said, "it's early. How long a drive to Salaverry?"

"Not so long. It depends on traffic. And with no cruise ship, there should not be much traffic in Salaverry today. Maybe one hour, maybe less."

"So, could you take us first to Chan Chan and wait for us while we see the ruins? Then continue on with us to Salaverry?"

"No problem."

"We must be in Salaverry to meet someone at four this afternoon. Can we see the ruins at Chan Chan and still get to Salaverry on time?" I asked.

"Oh, yes, you will have lots of time. It is early now. You should see Chan Chan and be in Salaverry for lunch, I think."

We settled on a fare. I paid the driver half of the agreed amount. "The rest when we reach Salaverry," I said and I offered him a tip if he served us well. *Más una propina.*

And serve us well he did. His vehicle was comfortable, and we soon arrived at the Chimu culture ruins of Chan Chan. We spent an hour there. The ruins were impressive. Different from Tiahuanacu but equally awesome and outshining anything else I had seen in Bolivia. Made of clay, the structures with their elaborate bas relief sculpturing had survived for more than one thousand years because it almost never rains in this dry, dry desert area. Even the original painting was well-preserved in many places. Gonzalo and I were awed.

It was midday when our taxi arrived in Salaverry. Entering Salaverry we passed many cargo containers and structures that I thought might be warehouses. "This is more than a port for cruise ships," I said to the taxi driver.

"Oh, yes," he replied. "This is the major port for Trujillo. It is one of Peru's busiest ports. Much freight comes into the country here."

We arrived at the waterfront where a low *malecon* (sea wall) separated the paved road from the beach about eight feet below the roadway. The beachfront road was no more than about two blocks long. Hotels, restaurants, and shops offering beach and surfing items dominated the roadway facing across the pavement toward the sea. At the end of the beach there was a wooden pier. It looked old. In fact, it looked like it might collapse at any moment. Hundreds, maybe thousands, of pelicans were roosting on it. Surely not the cruise ship pier.

Along the beach there were more than a dozen reed boats. They were unlike the reed boats on Lake Titicaca. Made of reeds, but squared off at the stern end. It seemed to me that one of them might be half of a Titicaca reed boat. A few were in the water and apparently being used by fishermen who were casting nets from them. Most were stacked against the *malecon*, resting on their sterns with prows upwards. At the far end of the beach were three open aluminum boats—bass boats, they are sometimes called in Ohio, I thought. They seemed both out of place and more practical for fishing than the truncated reed boats.

Our driver pulled to a stop at the Vista del Mar Hotel. I paid him the agreed fare, adding a tip of about five percent. "That's too much," said Gonzalo. "You don't tip taxi drivers here."

"Well," I said. "He was good for us, and we have lots of money."

"*Loco,*" commented Gonzalo.

Entering the hotel, we greeted the woman in charge and presented our passports. "Oh, yes," she said, "*Señores* Morrison and Masterson. We are expecting you. We have two rooms reserved, small rooms, I'm afraid. We are a small hotel. The rooms are upstairs and in the rear of the building. They will be quiet. Of course," she added, "every place in Salaverry is quiet. Except when a cruise ship docks on the other side of the town. Salaverry would like to be a center for surfing, but that has never happened. We have the waves, I guess, but nobody comes to ride them."

"The men with the reed boats?" I asked.

"They fish," she said. "And they will offer to take you for a ride. But you should be in a wet suit if you do that. It would be very wet, and the water here is cold."

"We need to find lunch," I said.

"The restaurant next door is not bad. It's the best that Salaverry has to offer."

After lunch we walked up and down the short street looking at shop windows. Then we climbed up on the *malecon* and sat side by side, looking out at the sea.

"I guess we have to wait a couple of hours," Gonzalo said. "Our contact is supposed to meet us here at four."

"Well, it's not yet four," a woman said behind us, "but I'm here."

We spun around. "Rosa Maria," Gonzalo exclaimed. "What? I mean how? How did you get here? Oh, it's good to see you!" Gonzalo jumped to the ground. He gathered Rosemary into his arms, embracing her. Then kissed her. Turning to me, he said, "Did she tell you we are engaged? We had planned to be married next month."

"Well, I'll be damned! I knew…. But I didn't know that you two—"

"And I didn't tell you," Rosemary said. "There were—still are, I guess—so many uncertainties in this escape plan, that I thought it best to say nothing. You didn't need the complication of worrying about our engagement."

"Well, will you stay here tonight? Let's get you checked into the hotel. There don't seem too be many people here. I'm pretty sure they'll have a room for you."

"I've already checked in," Rosemary said. "As Mrs. Morrison. Why do you think I reserved separate rooms for you guys?"

"Good. Okay, of course," I said. "Do you now tell us what to do? What will happen? Do you have our instructions?"

From her purse, Rosemary produced a sealed envelope with Gonzalo's name on it. "This came in this week via the diplomatic pouch. I have not opened it. As I told you, Paul, secrets are not always secret at the embassy. So it was sealed when it arrived, and it is still sealed."

She gave the envelope to Gonzalo. He tore it open. "Beach. ten A.M. Wednesday."

36

ROSEMARY AND I stood on the road beside the *malecon*. Gonzalo was with us, his backpack slung over one shoulder. A helicopter appeared out over the ocean, its noise building as it raced toward us. It swept low, the air wash from its blades scattering sand and trash. We looked up. People appeared around us, the local shopkeepers and other citizens, curious about this unusual event. A young boy near where we stood called out "Wow!" Wow it was, I thought, for the residents of Salaverry had certainly never seen anything like this—never anything this dramatic.

The helicopter had United States Navy painted on its sides. It made three passes over us, and then moved out to sea. Not far, perhaps a hundred yards, it seemed to me. As it flew over us, Gonzalo jumped down from the *malecon* and engaged in an earnest conversation with one of the boatmen. Gonzalo passed over some *soles* to him. Then, hurriedly, they ran to one of the beached aluminum boats. Pushed off and in the water, the Peruvian boatman started the boat's outboard motor and slowly headed out away from the beach. Once well away from the shore, the boatman cut the motor. Gonzalo stood up in the boat. The helicopter approached and hovered in place. A ladder dropped down, and a woman in military fatigues climbed down to the boat. An American Navy SEAL, I thought. With her help, Gonzalo climbed up and into the helicopter. She followed him, and the helicopter was soon out of sight.

"You did it!" Rosemary exclaimed and embraced me. "Now let's see if we can get a taxi to take us back to the airport at Trujillo. We don't need to stay around here."

In the taxi I asked, "What is next for you?"

"I return to Washington next week," she said. "I plan to resign from the CIA and join Gonzalo."

"Where will he be?

"In Cleveland, I believe. He has to study to take the examinations and then do an internship and residency before he can practice in the US. We'll get married soon, and you must be the best man."

"Okay," I said. "I look forward to that happy occasion."

"And so do I!" she responded.

"You should find a place to live in the Tremont neighborhood in what we call 'the near west side.' That's where most of the city's Hispanic population lives. Gonzalo should be able to get good internship training at Cleveland's Metropolitan General Hospital near there. They'll be glad to have him, and his Spanish will be a welcome asset. Of course, most of the Cleveland Hispanics are from Puerto Rico. And we would welcome Gonzalo into our pulmonary fellowship at University Hospitals for his second required year."

"He will need two years?"

"Yep. I'm afraid so. The internship will be demanding—long hours. But the second year as one of our fellows should be easy for him. He knows it all already."

At the airport we managed to get seats on a flight to Lima. In Lima, Rosemary booked a connecting flight back to La Paz; I secured a ticket to Miami on the American Airlines night flight. I checked into the Westin Hotel at the airport; I wanted a room in which to rest before flying to Miami.

With some time to spare, Rosemary and I found seats in the Westin's ground floor bar. I ordered a martini; she, white wine. We talked further about Cleveland and opportunities for Gonzalo. Rosemary was obviously and genuinely excited about their future. Pensively, obviously reflecting and seemingly unsure about what she should be saying, she said, "Gonzalo has told me about his relationship with Jennifer."

"All of it?" I asked.

"Well, I think so. Including the pregnancy, anyway. I'm not sure how that may play out when we show up as a couple and get married. Do you know how Jennifer feels about Gonzalo?"

"Yeah, I guess I do. She opened up to me just before I left to come here."

"And?"

"And, she does not want to see Gonzalo. She told me that if he comes to the lab, she will hide. But, if he becomes established at MetroHealth Center and you find a place to live in that area, there really will not be much of a reason for him to visit my lab at University Hospitals. There's the whole city of Cleveland between Metro and UH. And, importantly, you must not let that relationship between Gonzalo and Jennifer interfere with or color in any way your relationship with Gonzalo—and your start of a new life together with him."

Presently she rose, collected her things, and prepared to walk across the drive to the airport terminal. She turned to me. I embraced her warmly. "Thanks," she said. "I'll never be able to thank you enough." Then she strode out of the bar toward the terminal.

It was early morning when I arrived in Miami. I found a phone and called Susan.

37

MY LIFE IN CLEVELAND resumed quickly. I told Susan all about my adventures with Gonzalo. "We'll have to make him feel welcome here," she said.

"Yes," I said. "And I will call the folks at Metro Health Center to get him set up there. They'll be glad to have him."

"Okay. And I will take him and Rosemary shopping. He'll need clothes for sure. Maybe she will as well."

In the lab, Jennifer had kept things moving. It had only been a bit more than a week, I reflected to myself, and I had often been away at scientific meetings for times longer than this absence. The mail brought a five-year grant award notice. Dave Swenson had been true to his word.

Gonzalo and Rosemary found a second-story duplex apartment in Tremont not far from Metropolitan General Hospital. The Department of Medicine welcomed him there, moving him into the second-year residency rotations while calling it an internship.

Rosemary found a position as an interpreter at the hospital and joined Alice in teaching English as a Second Language at Pilgrim Congregational Church near the hospital.

I talked to the CWRU protestant chaplain, and he agreed to marry the couple in Harkness Chapel on the university campus. It was a simple but meaningful and poignant service, with Susan and me as their attendants. A few of his new hospital colleagues attended. Standing beside him, I noticed Jennifer sitting in the back row of the chapel sanctuary.

PART V

CULEBRA, PUERTO RICO, 2011

38

THE SIX-PASSENGER Vieques Airlink plane carried us over Flamenco Beach and between two hills before making an S curve down onto the runway at the Benjamín Rivera Noriega Airport on Puerto Rico's Culebra Island. The plane taxied to the small terminal building, and the propellers slowed to a stop as the pilot shut down the twin engines. While Susan waited for our luggage, I went to the Carlos Jeep Rental counter and rented a new and shiny Jeep. We drove out of the airport, turned right, and followed the highway for about a mile until we met a tree in the middle of the road, the pavement dividing into a lane on each side of the tree. We turned left, climbed uphill on the pot-hole-ridden road and descended again to Tamarindo Beach. Passing the beach, we reached Tamarindo Estates, where we had rented one of the twelve one-bedroom units for the next two weeks. We had vacationed on Culebra many times, and we looked forward to this up-coming escape from another Cleveland snowy winter.

At breakfast the following Friday morning Susan suggested, "Let's snorkel at Melones Beach this morning. There is almost no wind today. It should be good there, and we really should take advantage of a calm day. If we put it off to another day and the wind comes up, then Melones is not good for snorkeling."

"Sounds great to me," I said. "I'll make the bed, if you'll do the dishes. Then we can be off."

We drove into Dewey, the small town on Culebra, and turned right toward the dock. Just past the Catholic church we turned right and climbed up the hill past the medical clinic. Then down the steep hill to Melones Beach and the small town park there.

Usually quiet and unoccupied, Melones Beach was obviously the scene of some event this morning. This was not an ordinary, sleepy, Puerto Rican morning. People were gathered at a spot at the edge of the parking area just at the bottom of the hill. Many were talking; some seemed excited about something. We walked over to see what was happening. There, to our great surprise, was Gonzalo and with him, Rosemary. Kneeling on the ground, Gonzalo was splinting the arm of a boy maybe twelve years old.

"When he fell off of his skateboard he broke his wrist," Gonzalo said to a woman who was evidently the boy's mother. "I am splinting it, but he will have to go to the Caribbean Medical Center in Fajardo to have it properly set and secured in a cast. We'll get him on the next flight to Fajardo. Do you have a car to drive to the airport?"

"No," she said. "Well, we do, but it won't run now. It needs repairs that we cannot get done here on Culebra. And without those repairs, we cannot drive it to the ferry to take it to Fajardo. So no, we do not have a car. Or a car that works."

"My wife and I can drive him and you to the airport to catch the next flight to Fajardo."

"Can't we take the ferry tomorrow?" the woman asked. "It's much cheaper."

"No, I'm afraid not" Gonzalo said. "But after it is properly set and casted, you could stay overnight in Fajardo and return on the ferry tomorrow. But getting the bone properly aligned should be done right away, not tomorrow."

"We have cousins there with whom we can stay. We stay with them when we go to Fajardo to shop."

Looking up, Gonzalo spotted Susan and me. "Paul, Susan, what are you doing here? I mean, welcome to Culebra. It's great to see you, but how—"

Susan smiled and said, "Well, what are you doing here? We didn't expect to see you two here. We're vacationing. In fact, we've come to Culebra a number of times. Not every year, but fairly often. And we certainly didn't expect to find Dr. and Mrs. Mamani here."

Initially Susan and I had kept in touch with Gonzalo and Rosemary while they were in Cleveland. But they had their lives and we ours, and so we had drifted away from one another. We were embarrassed now that we had not kept up with our friends.

"Look," I said, "you need to take care of your patient. Dinner tonight at Barbara Rosa's? Our treat. How about it?"

"Sounds fun," Rosemary said, "but you should be our guests here on Culebra."

"Not at all, but you can bring some beer—Medalla."

"Great."

Eating fried shrimp at Barbara Rosa's front porch restaurant and enjoying the Puerto Rican beer, we heard the Mamanis' story.

"Well," Gonzalo said, "after I passed the USMLE exam for licensing and finished my year of internship at Cleveland Metropolitan General Hospital, I stayed on there in general medicine for a second year rather than join you at University Hospitals."

"Yes, I was disappointed in you for that," I commented.

"Then I started looking for practice opportunities. But first, some vacation for the two of us. That was important. And having heard about Culebra from some of my Puerto Rican patients in Cleveland, we decided to take our break here."

"We loved it on first sight," interjected Rosemary.

"They had no doctor, and the population won't really support one. Even with Medicare and Medicaid. The island is just too small," said Gonzalo. "Not enough people living here to support a full-time medical practice. But," he continued, "my years in the spy business have left me with enough money to live very comfortably for more years than I expect to be around.

"So now I am the island's doctor, and Rosa Maria the island's nurse. There is a small clinic—you passed it on the way to Melones Beach—where we see patients. There are four beds there, where we can keep an occasional patient overnight. But I don't like to do that. Sick people should be flown to Fajardo.

"We are part of the community now. We live in the *barrio*

(neighborhood, commonly used on Culebra for a particular hill-side neighborhood). Rosa Maria is on the town library board."

"So here we are," added Rosemary. "And in another seven months there will be another one of us!"

"Fantastic, wonderful!" Susan responded, with a warm, wide smile.

Driving back to Tamarindo Estates after dinner, Susan commented, "This story, their story, your espionage caper story, couldn't have a happier ending."

AUTHOR'S NOTES

This novel is a work of fiction. All of the characters in it are products of my imagination. Evo Morales was, in fact, president of Bolivia at the time Parts I, II and IV are set, and he still is as of this writing. He is the only historical person in the book. However, any actions, policies, or programs attributed to him are fictional. The Bolivian National Security Agency (Agencia Nacional de la Seguridad Boliviana, ANSEB) described in Part IV is fictional. I do not know if an agency of this type exists in Bolivia. If such an entity does exist, I have no knowledge of it.

I have lived in Bolivia and traveled extensively in both Bolivia and Peru. I have been to all of the places described in this book, from Suapi to Salaverry, from Coroico to Culebra. To the best of my ability, I have accurately described all of the sites in which this novel is set, although in many cases I have relied on decades-old memories. Many of the events described in Part II are drawn directly from my experiences in 1970–71. The Hotel Europa in La Paz is new since my last visit to Bolivia; the Gran Hotel Bolivar in Lima is described as I remember it. Other hotels in Puno and Cuzco are fictional.

I give thanks to many persons who have read drafts of my manuscript. Their comments have made this a better book. I especially thank my wife, Janet; my daughter, Ginnie; my brother, John Daniel; and my friends, Margaret Fissinger and Patricia Eldredge.

I have chosen to write in the first person. The protagonist in this work is, in fact, an individual such as I was during my biomedical career—an academic research scientist studying immune responses in persons with tuberculosis. Some of the studies described in Part II are drawn directly from work done by me and my colleagues. On the other hand, Dave, Jennifer, Gonzalo, Rosa Maria, and the Quispes are entirely fictional; they are not based on any persons known to me.

That the world's major sources of lithium ore are in Bolivia, China, and North Korea is, in fact, true.